OF COGS & CONJURINGS

THE WATCHERS OF ASTARIA, BOOK ONE

PATRICK DUGAN

Praise for Storm Forged

"Storm Forged is a superhero coming of age story with a truly innovate structure for both power and politics."

-*Hugo & Nebula Award-Winning Author Seanan McGuire*

Praise for Fate & Flux

"I was totally swept away by this story! Once I picked it up, I couldn't stop until I finished it."

Praise for Unbreakable Storm

"This second book in the series is even better than the first. I couldn't put it down. "

To my wonderful family, Hope, Emily, Nicholas, and Blaze. Thank you for all your love and support.

With a loud shriek of metal on metal, the last of my former living area collapsed from the side of the workshop forty feet to the ground. I eased myself over to the edge of the workshop and peered over the edge. Next to the massive tree trunk that supported my workshop, the metal frame shattered like an overheated knife. It had once been a small bedroom and storage closet. While not part of my duties as a Watcher, this was when my personal kind of fun began.

I adjusted my metal arm, making sure the straps were tight before starting on the next portion. An impervious arm worked great in a fight or blacksmithing, but normal people didn't have to worry about having an arm drop off if the straps failed. The receptor ends in the cup that held the stump of my right arm allowed me to throw lighting and fire blasts when I used my combat arm, not that either would help with this operation.

The new structure would become the kitchen and my living quarters. I'd assembled the addition's frame on the ground. Roland, my mentor, and the previous owner hadn't been much for comfort, but I needed a place to cook and sleep. He'd left me a series of books on the art of architecture. He insisted that these were the true masters and hacks like Bakker's treatise on building was garbage. Did I really need an addition? No, but if I was being honest with myself, the project kept my mind off Roland's death six months ago and all my failures.

"Master Quinn," Jabber called from down the hall. His metallic voice sounded raspy, meaning I'd need to tune his voice box gears again soon. Before I'd joined the Watchers, I'd always thought of automatons as golems, creatures created from magic that did the bidding of their masters. Most were machines, but Jabber was far more intelligent, knowledgeable, and…naggy. He could be a real mother hen at times, a quality not found in other golems I'd encountered. He was definitely more than a box of gears, and I had no idea how Roland had produced him. "I heard a crash. Is everything all right?"

"Yes, Jabber." Roland had named him such since he tended to never stop talking. "As I said earlier, I'm adding the new wing today."

"Wouldn't it be easier to use your magic?"

I turned to face him. He'd been constructed from bronze, which gave him a copper tint much like my own skin. He measured five and a half feet tall and was built like a lanky teenage boy instead of stout like most automatons. Roland had even added a bowler hat and a monocle for some reason I didn't understand.

"Sure. If my magic actually worked," I said, rolling up the plans, careful not to tear them with my metal hand. A wizard named Usorin had sliced my arm off in a fit of anger. In a way, I owed him for my current position. Roland had found me close to death, nursed me back to health, and built me a new arm. He'd also recruited me into the Watchers. Every silver lining had its cloud. "I've got the rigging all set up to raise the new addition."

"Very well, sir." Jabber returned to doing whatever he'd been doing before the commotion had distracted him.

I took the lift down to the small cabin below that hid the access point to Treetop from casual viewers. The cunning inner workings appeared to be part of the tree itself. Granted, being a day's travel from the closest town meant few passers-by—merchants bringing their wares to Braden-bridge or bandits—but an ounce of prevention and all that.

The camouflaged cabin held a small table, some game traps, and other features of a hunter's lodge. It had been ransacked a couple of times, but they'd never found the lift to upstairs or seen the workshop or stable thanks to spells Everard had done to conceal it. With the new coded lock I'd installed, they'd never get into the lift even if someone found it.

I pushed those thoughts from my brain, focusing on the task at hand. I'd hooked up guiding rigs and Roland's small airship to the add-on and hoped that would give me enough power. By myself, it would be tricky, but it wasn't like I had neighbors to come help me.

It was a calm day with a slight breeze. I'd only get one chance to attach the addition to the frame I'd built to hold it since I doubted it would look much different than the previous section if I failed. After double-checking the two winches I'd attached to the tree and the main lifting ropes under the airship, I fired up the furnace, watching the enve-lope enlarge as the steam-filled it with hot air. At a similar size to a lifeboat, it took a lot of steam to lift it.

Twenty minutes later, the airship I piloted bobbed over the structure below. I engaged the winches, lifting the struc-ture upon a series of pulleys affixed to supports above the destination. I shuddered at the groaning sound from the ropes as my new living quarters rose into the air. I'd computed the strain and found it within the safe range, but with any engineering project, you could never account for all the variables.

The minutes crept by as the new construction inched toward the rest of the structure forty feet above it. The airship rocked as I adjusted the fins to keep it steady. Adding to the challenge, the wind picked up, nudging the structure into a ponderous swing. A quick look at the sky made me sweat. Dark clouds scudded toward me.

The wind rocked the airship, bobbing it around like a twig on the sea. Of all the days for a storm to roll in. I needed another twenty minutes to get the piece in place and settled on the foundation and another half hour to secure the structure. From the looks of it, I didn't have that much time.

The airship was attached by ropes to the tree. I ran across the deck to check the tension on the ropes. The safety line would hold me, but I wasn't looking forward to the ride. I hooked my metal arm over the rope and slid down to the tree, dropping the last couple of feet to the workshop. I ratcheted up the winches. The smell of burnt rope and grease filled the area as the strain intensified on the steam engine that powered the rig. The add-on bucked and swayed. The pace and wind increased. While I understood Roland's decision to hide his workshop in the treetops instead of on the ground like a normal person, it made projects like this a lot more difficult.

The add-on hung over the support structure now, ten feet from success. I'd planned in using the airship to nudge it into place, but hard drops of rain pelted me as I climbed along a support beam. At the end of the structure, I used the strength of my mechanical arm to pull, dragging the add-on toward me. With my legs wrapped around the strut, I shimmied back, guiding the piece.

"I've got this," I said as I continued to move the addition.

Yet another gust of wind struck the Treehouse and addition alike, knocking me from my perch. My stomach lurched from the sudden acceleration. The ground sped toward me before I caught myself. I clutched the edge, dangling over a forty-foot drop. It seemed a lot closer now than it had before. The straps around my chest slipped as the weight came full on my metal arm.

Well, hells. I was either about to lose my arm—or myself. The connection with my stump separated, locking my fingers into place. My body swayed dangerously, held to my arm by the leather harness. I kicked desperately, swinging like an idiot until I grabbed hold of the metal frame with my left hand.

The rough metal tore at the skin, and blood made my grip slippery. Without the leverage of my right arm, I couldn't pull myself to safety. My brain raced as I tried to think of a way to not fall to my death.

"Jabber!" I screamed trying to force the panic out of my voice. I failed. No answer. The only time the automaton wasn't around.

"I'm sure the mighty engineer has everything well in hand if you'll pardon the pun, but might I be of service?" a voice called from the ground below me.

I glanced down, wishing I hadn't. Everard, the Arch Magus of all of Astaria and the head of the Watchers, stood with a wicked smirk on his face. He wore a red cloak over his leather jerkin.

"I can come back if this isn't an opportune moment." He laughed while I swung from my less than useful arm.

"Help!" I yelled. I hated to admit it, but I was in a bad spot.

"As you wish," Everard said.

I wondered if it would be less embarrassing to die.

2

Everard helped me into the workshop, and I connected the new partition to the original structure. I needed to hook up the water to run the kitchen and bathroom, but that would have to wait. Jabber might have cleaned the blood from Roland's bedroom, but... I still couldn't force myself to go into his space.

"You certainly are ambitious," Everard said as he walked through the addition. "How are you coming with your magic?"

Fire crept up my face. Over the past few months, I'd been driven to complete the living space and hadn't spent much time practicing magic.

"I see," Everard said before I could make up a good excuse. "Lady Maelyrra gave you magic so you could protect Astaria, not so you could squander it building your fortress and hiding from the world."

"It's not a fortress," I said with a bit more sulk in my voice than I liked. Roland's murder had shaken me to the core, and I'd neglected my duties as a Watcher as I convinced myself the new workshop had to have better quarters if I was going to be able to perform at an adequate level.

In reality, the magic eluded me. I couldn't even do the basic spells Everard, a mage who'd burned an entire army to ash, had taught me. Spells that were merely warm-up exercises, not the more useful enchantments. Who cares if I could rattle a glass or burn a piece of paper? Practicing the magic I supposedly possessed was a frustrating, humiliating experience.

Everard sighed, taking a seat on the floor. The Arch Magus gestured for me to join him. I dropped down and across from him. He didn't say anything for a few moments. "I know this is hard on you, Quinn. You've lost more than most people do in a lifetime, but I need you, and more importantly, Lady Maelyrra requires your protection."

"Why would she need me for anything?" I asked. The whining tone in my voice sparked a throb of guilt knowing in the six months since Roland died and I received my magic I'd done nothing. "She's more powerful than any of us. She could destroy anyone who threatened Astaria in a heartbeat. For that matter, we could hand out enough alarium-powered devices to the magus to fight anyone who attacks."

"No," the Arch Magus said, shaking his head. "Maelyrra is bound to her realm and only ventures here at great cost. She grants a mage magical powers to protect Astaria and the alarium that holds the magic. Only you and I have real magic"

"Don't you mean magus?" I asked, assuming he'd misspoken.

"No. Mage is a person who has true magic. Magus is a title and gives the bearer the right to the alarium-powered devices that conceal when we don't have more magic at our disposal."

My jaw dropped as what the older man said registered. "How are alarium and magic related?"

"The magic we tap into is contained in the alarium beneath Astaria. Once it's gone, the magic will cease. It's why we mine so little of it."

"What?" Like most of Astaria, I had been raised to believe that the magus were magic users and they ruled because of that power. After Roland brought me in, I learned that alarium devices were the true power.

"I guess I should have explained things more thoroughly. If the Candalarians or the Norns realized there were vast veins of the precious metal that we hadn't tapped, they would seek to destroy them to eliminate our magic."

"Why? They have magic of their own."

"Norn magic is derived from death. They sacrifice people to fuel their resurrection magic."

"And the Candalarians?"

"They tap into the energy of the spirit realm to power their spells. It's unreliable but powerful in the hands of a trained Walker."

"Walker?"

He smiled at me. "I forget how new you are to all of this. The Wind Walkers are the mages of the Candalarians. They convert spiritual energy into magic."

"Oh." Every time I thought I had a basic understanding of the world, I found out more I'd not been told. Why had Roland picked me to be a Watcher? I knew nothing beyond the forge. Maelyrra had wasted her magic on a one-armed blacksmith. After six months, I couldn't move a mote of dust with magic. Sure, I could build alarium powered weapons and items for the other Watchers, but I'd never fulfill the responsibility she'd laid at my feet.

"Enough on the topic for today, though we will obviously

need to discuss your formal training soon," Everard said with a pointed look. "We have a situation I need you to deal with."

"Are the Norns back?" I asked. I'd fought their leader and killed him. I'd left him roasting like a gutted pig on a forge fire.

"No, nothing that large, but there have been incursions into the Aldon region. Something has attacked two villages. The Watcher there, Aurelia Salwey, was killed in the first attack on Herot's Pass," he said, pulling out a map to consult. It showed the thirteen regions of Astaria, each with a Lord Magus to lead and a Watcher to take care of issues Everard wanted handled. From Terralon far to the north all the way down to Aldon in the south. Everard's finger stabbed the map. "Herot's Pass and Murkwood reported their inns destroyed the day after magus Quiliel of Aldon made his quarterly visit. He hasn't had any luck locating the perpetrators. Honestly, the man is an imbecile and couldn't find his butt with both hands and a map."

"Sounds like a great leader," I said dryly. "What do you need me to do?"

Everard shot me a mirthful glance. He did his best to tolerate magus' royal tendencies. "You'll be meeting up with Cian, the Watcher from Ramcoll, in Murkwood. He's an experienced ranger so he'll be of use in tracking down whatever is killing people."

"Whatever?" I wasn't sure whether giving me help was a vote of no-confidence or the situation was worse than I thought.

"There weren't a lot of witnesses to the deaths. In both cases, the inn was attacked, and all the inhabitants were killed. The timing troubles me. It seems beyond circumstance that the towns are assaulted the day after the magus left. According to Quiliel, a boy saw a monster."

"A monster? What kind of monster?"

"I don't know, but we need to find out what is happening. Aldon borders the Candalarian territories which always makes it more important." He shook his head. "Astaria is in greater danger than I've ever seen. The Norns are building more ships, and the Candalarians have been gathering the horse clans at Thaclet. The magus leaders are demanding more alarium weapons to protect them from the threats."

"Why me? If Cian is a ranger, won't he be able to track the people responsible?"

"He probably could," Everard said, rubbing his forehead with the palm of his hand. "You need field experience. You've handled your artificer responsibilities well, but you need to be a complete Watcher."

"You mean murdering people that piss you off?"

Everard glared. "That is a small part of the job, but yes it sometimes is required. More often your missions will be to protect the people of Astaria by any means necessary."

"And Roland sacrificing his life was just another necessity?"

"It was unfortunate and I was far closer to him than anyone else. I know he explained the risks to you. Are you walking away from the Watchers? Does Roland's death mean that little to you?"

I shook my head. "No, I swore an oath to Roland and I'll not let him down. I still don't like your methods."

"We do what is needed to ensure the people of Astaria are protected, even the ones we don't like."

"I guess we better get started. Something is killing our people and I mean to stop them." I didn't add if I could to the end.

I wondered if I was strong enough to stop the killing or if I'd be joining Roland in the afterlife.

3

The smell of blood, fire, and death clung to the dank night air like scale forge to a piece of molten iron. Behind us smoldered the burning remains of a small farmhouse, and behind that, the remains of the family who had lived there. The fire didn't look intentional, but the people had all been torn to shreds. My guess was the fire got out of control as they tried to scare off the bear.

It turned out the kid from Murkwood had been right. The perpetrator of the attacks was a monster. Now all I needed to do was figure out who was creating them.

The moon peeked out between the roiling clouds as the wind picked up from the west. My leather mask with specially created optics enhanced the dim light, making it easier to see. It also protected our identities since Watchers tended to make powerful enemies. I adjusted my cloak and moved out into the night. Cian scouted ahead, searching for a trail to follow.

Lapis, a small town on the southeastern coast of Astaria, was our destination. According to Cian, it was a sleepy village nestled in the hills overlooking the sea. Thatch huts and broad-beamed buildings housed the town of two hundred or so, and nothing had ever happened here to put the town into the history books besides its incorporation.

I cleared my mind, picturing the monster as it had been described to me by the Murkwood boy who'd survived its last attack. Once Cian and I stopped the killing, there would be time to find who was behind these atrocities.

I pulled the tuft of fur I'd retrieved from the Murkwood attack and concentrated. I crossed my hands in front of me and said the words Everard had taught me to cast a finding spell.

"Dilna op nata." I spread my hands wide, tossing the fur into the wind.

Nothing happened. I retrieved the fur, tried again.

Frustration and irritation flared hot when the spell failed a second time. After two more attempts, I gave up, stuffed the remaining fur in my pouch, and waited for Cian to return from scouting for the trail.

Magic was effortless for Everard, but I'd been more successful at the forge than casting any spells. Maelyrra might have given me magic after I'd stopped Orvo from stealing it through the machine he'd created, but the power wouldn't respond to me. I followed Everard's instructions to a T, and nothing.

When I was given the magic, I'd been able to feel it inside me like the heat from the sun. When I cast spells, I might as well have been taking a nap I felt so empty.

I found a stump and took a seat. Might as well be somewhat comfortable while the ranger sought traces of our prey. I pushed up my Watcher mask and looked at the stars. Was Roland up there, guiding me? I could almost hear him telling me, "Get a move on, lad." Without him, I'd have been a one-armed man with no prospects beyond begging or robbery.

He'd saved my life and I'd let him down when he needed me. I'd failed my family, my mentor, Everard, and Lady Mylerra. The least I could do was save the Astarian people from this unnatural predator. I refused to fail my oath as a Watcher, even if it killed me.

My mask had smudges on the eyepieces, so I pulled a cloth out and carefully cleaned them. A marvel of ingenuity, their lenses compensated for both darkness and bright light. They protected our identities from the public so we could move about without being harassed in our real lives. The mouth slit filtered out dust and toxins.

Once the lenses gleamed, I checked the status of the enhancements I'd made on the mask since Roland had died. I might not be able to cast spells, but I could improve on the designs Roland had created, at least.

"I found the trail," Cian called, striding across the field. I adjusted the secondary chest strap that helped to hold my arm in place, which I had designed after the embarrassing incident with Everard a few days ago.

"Let's go," I replied. Cian led the way to some trampled grass and other markings of the bear's passage. One thing was sure, Cian was an amazing tracker. "Follow my directions when we confront the monster."

Cian frowned at me before scouting the area for more signs. "How in the hell did we get a monster out here?"

I increased my stride to keep up with the taller man. "I don't know, but from the little I've heard it is at least partially mechanical."

"An abomination is what that is," he said, his gaze flickering over the ground in front of us. We made steady progress over the uneven terrain, on the trail of our quarry. "Thing has to be twice the size of a horse, given the prints."

I swallowed hard. I'd faced off against men and machines,

but never a creature the size Cian described. "How far behind are we?"

Cian stopped, knelt, and studied one of the immense paw prints that were mostly hidden by the clumps of grass around it. I knelt beside him, examining the deep impression in the ground. I hadn't noticed the print before he pointed it out.

Cian traced the outline with his finger. "I wouldn't think too far. See how the print is pressed into the soft dirt, but there is only a bit of water? After a few hours, the groundwater will seep in to fill the depression."

I cleared my throat. "We should pick up the pace. I don't want any more people killed by this thing." Bile rose in my throat at the thought of finding more bodies tonight.

Cian snorted a laugh. "It already killed one Watcher. You're assuming we won't be part of the dead after going up against this monster. I've dropped a couple of big animals in my time, but nothing to rival this one. He must be over a thousand pounds."

However dangerous the threat—mechanized monsters, psychotic Norns, or rogue Magus—it was the job of the Watchers to protect the people of Astaria. Fear thrummed through my body in time with my hammering heart. Regardless, people were dying, and it was up to me to save them. So much for starting off with an easy mission. I wished I could have stayed hidden like I had since Roland was murdered six months ago.

Over the next hour, we followed the trail of the giant bear across the rolling hills. Luckily, we didn't happen across any more farms or other folks the bear had visited. The moon shone brightly overhead, making it easier to move quickly. As we crested the top of the largest hill yet, the quiet town of Lapis appeared in front of us.

It was not so quiet this evening. The villagers had built a

long bonfire across the road leading into the hamlet. I pushed my mask into place and the scene illuminated as the goggles enhanced my sight. Dead bodies and farm implements dotted the ground around a massive bear who lurked a short way away from the barricade. So much for a monster. The bear had mechanical eyes and armor platting. Obviously, the villagers had charged the monster and hadn't fared well. I'd heard the descriptions, but I wasn't prepared for just how massive this beast was.

Shadows flickered around the flames, making the illuminated faces of the villagers look contorted in its light. The tension in the air could be cut with a knife.

A bestial roar shattered the still night air. The bear lumbered toward the town, trampling the corpses as it went.

"We've got to get there." I set off at a run, only to be halted by Cian's barked order, louder due to his Watcher's mask.

"Stop!"

I skidded to a halt and gestured impatiently. The people of Lapis weren't armed to take on such a huge foe. For that matter, nothing in my blacksmith training had prepared me for this. Roland had taught me the basics of fighting, though my education was far from complete. "People are going to die if we don't stop that monstrosity."

Cian jogged to my side, down the slope of the hill. "Quinn, use your head. Run the whole way and you'll be too tired to fight. The fire will hold the bear back until we get there and draw the animal off."

I hated to admit it, but he was right. "Fine, but we need to get there quickly."

Cian grinned before settling his mask in place and setting off at an easy pace. I tried not to fall flat on my face as the uneven footing threatened to trip me. If the townspeople occupied the bear for ten minutes or so, I could use my armaments to drive it to a safe distance before we killed it.

A bolt of lightning streaked from behind the fire into the approaching bear. Lightning, and not the natural sort. Another of the blue-white streaks followed.

Was that Magus Quielel, the ruler of Aldon? I increased my pace, which Cian easily matched. With a Magus on hand, we'd have more firepower, but alone he was vulnerable.

The bear stood on two legs, bellowing its challenge. Arcs of blue-white lightning crackled around the beast. The strikes did little damage to the armor but seriously irritated the bear. With an earsplitting roar, its front legs came down and it charged the magus, absorbing the lightning strikes with no sign of slowing.

The barrier of flame burst as the monstrosity drove through it, sending villagers screaming away from their attacker. Magus Quielel stood his ground.

Cian and I got there in time to see the bear's massive jaw clamp down on the magus' head. Blood spurted in all directions as the animal shook the corpse until the body tore free, landing in a pile at its feet. The head bounced across the ground.

We slowed to a halt, panting. The bear grasped the headless corpse and began to drag it away from the fire. I readied my arm and gauntlet for the fight. The glow from the alarium shimmered around my arms. I turned to Cian. "Do bears eat humans?"

He shook his head, as bewildered by the spectacle as I was. "No, not usually."

The bear lifted a massive paw and struck repeatedly at the corpse. "What is it doing?"

"I've no idea." Cian pulled his hood up over his head. He gestured back toward the fire. "We've got other problems, though."

I followed his gaze. The town's people were dissolving into a panicked mob. Some ran for cover, others thought to challenge the monstrosity that had killed their neighbors. Some carried farm implements, others flaming torches, but they were determined to fight. The bear ignored them dragging the corpse along the ground.

So much for this being an easy mission.

17

4

S creams of anger and fear erupted from the villagers. Women and children rebuilt the barricade fire, sending sparks off into the darkness. The men, determined to save their families from the beast, braced for a fight and shook pitchforks and hoes, a few shoving long torches into the fire.

From our vantage point just outside the firelight, we watched the bear tear an arm free from the Magus and set it aside. "What is he doing?" Cian asked while we watched the morbid display.

I shook my head, having no idea myself. "Do we just leave him be and wait for him to move off?"

Arrows tipped with flame rained down on the bear, bouncing harmlessly off the armor. One lucky shot found a weak point and sunk its barbed head into meaty shoulder flesh. The animal roared in pain before charging toward the town. Shrieks of terror sounded as the giant plowed into the fire again, sending burning logs skittering like dice at the local tavern.

We headed toward the carnage. The angry animal swatted

anyone within reach, throwing them like rag dolls. The fire had wisely been built far away from the majority of Lapis's buildings. Otherwise, the whole place might have burnt down.

Cian outpaced me, his long legs covering more ground than I could ever hope to. He became a blur in the shadows. Pistols appeared in each hand as he fired at the beast's head.

A few moments later I reached the fight. Cian danced around the monster like one of those fancy acrobat performers. He flowed in circles around the attacker, firing into the massive body over and over again. The tang of the projectiles striking armor filled the air.

"Stop!" I yelled at the townspeople, backing them off from the bear.

"I'll keep him busy, you figure out how to stop him," Cian yelled as he continued harassing the bear. A series of shots pinged off the armored bear. As with any great plan, it fails once the fighting starts.

The bear ignored Cian and spun toward me. His mechanical eyes twisted to focus on me. How I was supposed to stop a rampaging gigantic bear?

First I'd need to be close enough to strike it. I dashed into the melee, throwing a ball of flame from my mechanical arm. With a yell, I hiked up my shield and blocked one huge swipe. The bear continued the onslaught. Its claws sparked as they raked the alarium generated field. The force of the blow shoved me across the clearing. After an awkward landing, I collapsed to the ground in an undignified heap.

Cian's guns fired at the animal, ricocheting off into the night.

The bear reared on his hind legs, lurched forward, and heaved itself atop me, attempting to crush me beneath its massive frame. Or it almost did. I rolled away from the blow. Could my shield could absorb the force of that much weight?

The bear continued its pursuit, now focused on me and nothing else. Clambering to my feet, I backpedaled away from another slashing blow. I didn't see Cian, but then again, the bear took up most of my field of vision. I tried to outmaneuver my foe, but a piece of log tripped me. I went down hard as the bear pounced.

My shield held as the animal's incredible bulk pinned me to the ground. White cracks appeared in the blue energy as claws fought for purchase. When the shield failed, the bear would smash my head like an overripe pumpkin.

A flash of flame appeared above us, and the bear staggered to the side. Cian shoved the burning branch closer to the animal, giving me a chance to stand. I scrambled away, flicking off the shield before the damage overloaded the alarium core.

"Did you shoot his mother?" Cian yelled as I increased the charge to my lightning attack. The bear stopped in its tracks with its head at an odd angle as if it was listening to us speak. "He seems to be on a mission to eat you, my friend."

"No idea." This close, the optics that had replaced the bear's eyes glowed with a strange red light. "The real question is what are they trying to accomplish?"

"I see you don't share Roland's sense of humor."

The remark stung like I'd been shot. "Roland is dead. We've got to handle this our way or we'll be joining him." I tried to keep the hurt and anger out of my voice but failed miserably. Any further comments were cut short by an ear-splitting roar the bear launched toward us.

Cian leapt to the left, firing his pistols at its flanks while I opened up with a burst of flame, scorching the fur around the bear's muzzle. It reared up and slammed back down, clipping me with dagger-like claws.

I took the blow on my metal arm and immediately wished

I hadn't. The new restraining strap popped, leaving my appendage hanging limp and numb at my side.

"Quinn!" Cian yelled over the roar of the angry grizzly.

I dodged left, holding my mechanical arm in place so the connections could reestablish. Without those, the arm was virtually useless. Feeling returned, much to my relief. I opened up with a barrage of fireballs, forcing the enraged beast back.

Cian appeared next to me. "What happened?" He fired a series of quick shots at the massive head, cracking one of the mechanical eye lenses.

"Strap broke. See if you can reattach it." The bear circled us cautiously now, and I tracked it as Cian knotted the broken strap.

"It won't take another blow, but it should hold until you can repair it."

I reached into my belt pack and grabbed my latest invention, the sonic bomb. "When I tell you to, push the button, throw it at the bear, and cover your ears."

Cian held the ball by a wire poking out of its bronze casing. "Is it going to sing off-key?"

Instead of answering, I charged the bear, firing two arcs of electricity from my reattached arm. The lightning wouldn't do anything to the animal, but if it momentarily blinded him, Cian's chances of a hit increased. "Now!"

The device bounced off the bear's snout before landing directly under it. A loud whistle erupted as the sonic blast reached its full potential. The bear shied away from it, giving me my opening. I leapt onto his back, my hands latching onto the strap holding his armor in place.

The response was immediate and terrifying. The beast roared and shook. My body swung wildly as I fought to hold onto the straps. He bucked uncontrollably, but I stuck to him like a hot weld.

The bear dropped to all fours, nearly jolting me off. The bear lumbered toward Cian, hardly slowed by the additional weight. The tracker danced just out of reach and kept the bear engaged so he wouldn't focus on ridding himself of his unwanted rider.

I worked furiously at the buckles. Success! Pieces of armor rained down as the plates were freed. The bear didn't appreciate my work. It jerked sideways, again unsuccessful in dislodging me.

We'd moved closer to the remains of the fiery barricade. The increased light revealed a piece of metal about the size of my hand embedded in the bear's fur between its shoulder blades. Tubes ran from the plate into the bear's body.

I wedged my fingers under the plate and pulled. Blood and a blue liquid spurted. I yanked what turned out to be a metal box out of the animal's flesh.

As soon as the wires broke, the bear dropped onto its belly dead. After a few moments, I leapt free, the box still in my hands. Cian joined me as I ran farther away.

A group of villagers charged to join us. The leader inclined his head. "Master Watchers, is the beast dead?"

Cian turned to them. "He's dead. The Watchers have done their duty."

A cheer went up, but no one else approached. The Watchers might save your village or they might arrive to dispense the Arch Magus' justice. The safe bet was to stay away, far away.

"Everard said you were in charge. What do we do now?" Cian asked once he made sure all the others had gone. He had a smile on his face and looked ready to fight again.

With a pop and the clanking of metal, my arm fell to the ground.

"I'm going to invent some better straps."

5

The sun was about to set as I pulled the cart with the supplies I'd purchased in Bradenbridge into the small barn that stood at the base of the massive tree that held home and workshop. The sigils Everard had used to hide the barn flared in my sight as I crossed through the hiding spell. At least I could see his magic now, that was an improvement.

When I'd first arrived at Treetop, the lift had been hidden, but after Roland's murder, I'd added a mechanical lock to guard against intruders. I moved the interlocking pieces until they clicked into place and the door slid open. Working methodically, I stacked each crate of supplies on the lift's floor until the cart was empty.

After I pressed the button for the upper floor, it shuddered and jerked to life, another thing I'd have to fix one day, but it worked for now.

"Good day, Master Quinn. I assume your mission was a success?" Jabber asked as I entered.

I handed a wooden crate full of vegetables to Jabber. "It was. Any word from Everard?"

"Indeed, there is a word." He followed behind me as I carried more supplies to the new kitchen. I hadn't had time to finish the build, but the shelves were mounted on the wall. For now, I'd rigged up a small burner for cooking.

I realized Jabber, who took questions literally, wasn't going to tell me what word we'd received from the Arch Magus. "Jabber, what did Everard say?"

"He said Watcher Atwater had reported in. He congratulated you on stopping the bear and directed you to find who is behind it. He also inquired on your magic and insists you come to Vario to continue your education."

I sighed, not wanting to think about magic, killer mechanically enhanced bears, or anything else. All I wanted to do was cook myself a large dinner and go to bed. I'd been on the road for over three weeks hunting the bear and now had more questions than answers. "Respond to Everard. Tell him I will be investigating the source of the box and will track down the perpetrator. Afterward, I'll be in Vario for training." Maybe.

It took a while to stash my provisions and cook butter-poached chicken and mashed potatoes for dinner. My cooking skills had increased during my solitude.

Jabber sat across from me at the table as I ate. had that been the automaton's habit when Roland lived here? "Jabber, how long did Roland live here alone?"

The automaton cocked his head as he processed the question. "Master Roland only came here to work or train apprentices. He did not live here as you have been."

I chewed the slightly overcooked chicken. "Where did he live?"

"Master Roland had a residence in River Cross. I do not have further details," Jabber answered. I'm sure he had details, but Roland would have locked them away in Jabber's memory.

"I didn't realize he had other apprentices." I'd been with Roland for a few months before the attack that killed him, but he'd never mentioned taking on other assistants. It still shocked me how much I didn't know about my mentor. He'd saved me after I'd lost my arm and I'd barely gotten to know him before he was murdered.

"Roland had three apprentices before you. Two have retired from the Watch. One was killed in an explosion."

"Explosion?"

"I do not have details of the mission, only the entry notifying the Arch Magus of the outcome of the mission."

"Interesting." I finished eating, cleaned up, and headed for bed. The next few days would be busy as I tried to decipher the metal box I'd torn out of the bear.

⁂

Three days later after disarming numerous traps, I finally opened the box without damaging the interior. Whoever built the device had wanted its secrets to die with the bear. They'd installed several small explosives and a vial of highly corrosive acid which I had removed before the attached explosives could trigger.

A wire casing fed into a small box covered in runes like the Norns or the Candalarian Hordes used to control their magic. Too bad shaman magic was as much a mystery to me as my own.

I set the box aside, checking out the series of gears attached to a syringe that pushed the blue liquid through the tubes. With a set of crimpers, I closed off the tube before I removed it. Luckily some of the fluid remained in the syringe. The gears were set to rotate at a small increment and deliver more of the fluid. How often and how much fluid was delivered would determine how long it had been since the animal had been with its creator.

The blue liquid-filled half the syringe. The big question still hadn't been answered. What did this do? How could I run tests to determine what it was? I needed an expert which was definitely not me

I rummaged through the tomes on the rebuilt shelves until I found a book of maps. I spread it out on the workbench and cranked up the alarium lamp. On the page showing the Alolon fiefdom, I traced the bear's progress from Lapis to Murkwood to Herot's Pass where the first known attack had occurred.

According to the map, Herot's Pass provided the best passage to the grasslands of Oriatia, though the forest and Kirfolk mountains certainly didn't lend itself to an easy trek. Most likely the bear had originated there, but you could hide a lot in the treacherous mountains.

Jabber entered carrying a steaming teapot and a cup. "I thought you could use a bit of refreshment, Master Quinn."

"Thank you, Jabber."

The automaton poured the tea and placed it near enough for me to reach, but away from my work. "Might I be of some assistance?"

"Only if you can identify what the liquid in the syringe is or what these runes mean," I said peevishly, waving my hand over the disassembled device. Three days of work and I barely knew more than I had before.

"I'm afraid not. Master Roland's notebooks contain the list of Watchers and their specialties."

"I hadn't thought to check there." The notebooks had been housed in the workshop, but Jabber relocated the books to Roland's old room while I repaired the workshop.

I hadn't been in his room since the day I'd found his body. The horrid images flashed before my eyes as I considered having Jabber fetch them. While the automaton could do a lot of things, reading Roland's atrocious handwriting left a lot of room for error.

Dread struck at my heart, but I had to do this. I opened the door to the musty smell of the unused room. Jabber had cleaned all the blood and viscera from the floor and burned the carpet, but my gaze was drawn immediately to the spot where Roland had been hung from his arms. I stood frozen in the doorway, unable or unwilling to enter the place where my mentor had been murdered. A rivulet of sweat dripped down my back as my anxiety climbed.

His oversized bed, nightstand, and the alarium core that powered Treetop occupied the back wall. A small desk and set of drawers stood off to the right. Bookshelves covered the left wall from floor to ceiling. Jabber had piled the workshop's library in front of the shelves. I swallowed the bile that threatened to climb up my throat and forced myself into the room.

Giving the center of the room a wide berth, I crouched in front of the first stack, searching for the notebook Jabber mentioned. Books full of alchemical and metallurgy theory, sketches of new inventions, and every message Roland had received from Everard were in the first pile. The other stacks on the floor were the same. Nothing.

Next, I examined the books on the shelves. More tomes on every possible subject filled these shelves. I didn't recognize most of the names, but I was surprised to find a copy of Bakker's treatise on architecture. What was this doing here? Roland had said Bakker was an idiot who didn't know the first thing about architecting a pigpen, let alone a building.

Curious, I pulled the book and heard a loud click. A section of bookshelf swung away from the wall, revealing a tiny hidden room.

Lights flickered to life as I stepped through the opening.

Roland's cloak and Watcher mask hung from a hook on the wall. A larger desk than the one in his bedroom was covered with papers and an enormous black book. The back wall held a metal plate the size of a shield. I pulled the steel handle to expose a hole that was deeper than the light in this room could penetrate. Hm.

I pulled a coin from my pocket and tossed it into the dark. The sound echoed as the coin bounced down what I guessed was a slide. Roland always had a plan, including a secret escape route from Treetop. I wished he'd used it that day instead of fighting.

I shut the hatch and took a seat in from of the desk. The book was open, face down. I flipped it over and saw Roland's familiar scrawl detailing the process he was using to double harden copper to increase its strength.

The other pages contained more drawings for completed projects. I paused at the familiar diagrams for a heating system, the one he'd built for Usorin. At the bottom in Roland's scrawl was written, "Keep an eye on Quinn." I'd never met Roland until the day he saved my life, so had he jotted down this note before or after I'd lost my arm? At this point, I'd probably never know.

With a huff, I turned the page, searching for the Watcher's list. No luck. I set it on the floor and rifled through the papers until I uncovered a small notebook. The Watcher's eye insignia graced the front cover, and inside was the list of Watchers.

Roland was listed as the Artificer for the Terralon territory under Usorin. I skimmed the other twelve entries. Atwater was noted as Ranger, as was someone named Brull, though his name was crossed off. An explosives expert, Doctor, and others were here, but alchemist was the one I needed. The name beside it was Wyndham and the region of Whitland. Thirteen districts and only eleven Watchers. How long since had the list had been updated? At least since Roland had started training me, I presumed, since my name was scribbled at the bottom with Artificer beside it.

Mission accomplished, I headed for the door when I noticed Roland's watch on the shelf. It stopped me in my tracks. As hard as it was, I tried to envision Roland in here instead of the corpse I'd found in the other room. I'd sworn to avenge his and all the other murders of the people I loved. After fruitless months of searching, I was no closer to finding Roland's killer, but the bill would come due one day no matter how long it took. One day the coward would rear his head again, and I'd be ready.

6

I spent the next week poring over reference books about the Candalarian Horde. The horse clans of the Verdant Plains were masters of hit and run raids on outlying settlements and traders. The southern Astarians called them the white ghosts since they were of pale complexion. I found volumes on fighting styles and culture, but only trace amounts of information regarding their magic.

Jabber interrupted an excruciatingly boring section of Cuttle's "Warlords of the Candalarian Hordes," much to my pleasure. The author stated facts but didn't connect them back to the actual people and how their ways impacted their society.

"Master Quinn, I contacted Watcher Wyndham as you requested via the telex. You are to meet in four days at the Broken Spoke in Stillhold. You will know the Watcher by an onyx stickpin in the lapel. You are expected at noon."

I nodded. My knowledge of geography outside of Terralon was sketchy at best since I hadn't left Bradenbride in the twenty-five years before becoming a Watcher. "Stillhold should only take a couple of days to get to."

"If you take the airship from Bradenbridge to Stillhold, you will reach it in three days, two to ride to Bradenbridge, one on the airship. Riding a horse from here would take four to five days, depending on how hard your push your mount. I'd suggest the airship."

I didn't respond to the obvious fact I'd just said as much. "Is there anything else I need to know about the meeting?"

"When you approach Watcher Wyndham, the passphrase will be 'What should you do with a dead chemist?' and the appropriate answer is 'barium.'"

What an awful joke. This Wyndham fellow was an odd cog for sure. "Thank you, Jabber. I'll leave in the morning."

Jabber didn't answer but stood there shaking. No, not shaking. Laughing. Since when did automatons have a sense of humor? Roland must have spent a great deal of time teaching Jabber.

"Barium...bury 'em," the automaton repeated to himself as he left.

⸎

I waited impatiently for noon to arrive before leaving my room at the Broken Spoke. The night before, I'd caught a ride from the airship to the inn with a steady wind whipping dust at my back. I'd had to use a makeshift mask to help me breathe. Stillhold was a farming community, but the bartender told me that in stopping the Norns, the magical battle had diverted the river that fed the town, leaving a dustbowl in its place.

After affixing my everyday arm, I clopped down the stained and scuffed oak stairs into the common room. This arm didn't have built-in weapons, preferring to not call attention to my absent arm or the weapons I carried to fight with. The onyx stickpin pierced the lapel of the coat I wore over my white shirt.

Once I reached the common room, I glanced around for any sign of Watcher Wyndham. A large fireplace dominated the wall to my right and the bar took up the left. A bored serving girl swabbed out wooden mugs with a cloth I wouldn't have cleaned my anvil with. I wouldn't be eating here if it could be helped. Twelve long tables filled the center of the room.

A couple of trappers in roughhewn clothes sat near the fire, laughing and swapping stories. The table held their drinks and two pairs of goggles with attached respirators. I wished I'd have known to bring the same with me. My Watcher's mask would handle the dust, but it would also mark me.

After examining the trappers, I concluded Watcher Wyndham wasn't a member of that party. Two men wearing bowlers and dark coats, and a woman wearing a coat, but no hat, sat near the door. While they appeared to be discussing business, the woman watched the door like a hawk while the other two sized me up in a not-so-friendly manner. None of them wore an onyx stickpin.

I took a seat on the other side of the room from the unfriendly group, closer to the trappers. The far door opened. As the air billowed across the room, making me realize I should have chosen a different table when the smell of the trappers reached me. All three of the tough's heads pivoted toward the open door.

A tall woman strode in, slamming the door behind her. Her long dust streaked coat nearly concealed her black shirt and pants. While it wasn't unheard of, a woman in pants still elicited scowls and comments. A respirator and goggles hung around her neck like an elaborate necklace. She scanned the room before walking straight toward me. "What do you do with a dead chemist?"

I groaned, still hearing Jabber's laughter ringing in my head. "Barium."

Yep. Onyx pin in her lapel. Before me stood Watcher Wyndham, alchemist, adventurer, and a woman. I'd have to inform Jabber. "I'm Quinn. Nice to meet you, Watc--"

She cut me off. "None of that. Didn't Roland teach you anything? Call me Victoria. Follow me." She pivoted on her heel and headed toward the front door. The trio had risen to block her path. I stepped up behind her.

"Master Spencer would like to have a few words with you, Lady Yorke." The lead man's smile never faltered as his hand went to the knife at his belt. The movement revealed hardened leather armor under his duster. The other two, the man with a long, greying beard and the woman had long dirty brown hair braided down her back. Both held short clubs in their hands. The woman's eyes darted toward me and back to Victoria, clearly nervous.

"Aren't you going to introduce your companions?" Victoria asked, her tone was more appropriate for a garden party.

Granville smirked. "Why of course. Allow me to introduce Miss Laurel Anne Hill," he gestured to the woman who nodded at us. "And Mr. Silas Tanner."

The older man grunted in response.

"A pleasure, I'm sure. Now if you allow me and my associate to pass, I'll bid you all a good day."

"All you'll be doing is coming with us to speak with Master Spencer," Granville said.

Victoria snorted a laugh. "Please, Granville. Jed Spencer has never been and never will be a master of anything. Run back to your boss and tell him his money is coming and not to bother me again."

Granville's smile turned feral. The knife slipped out of the sheath. "Laurel Anne, watch the door. Silas, take care of her friend." The ruffians flanked us. Silas, whose long grey beard hung halfway to his belt, came closer to me.

"Granville, you are making a serious mistake," she said softly.

"The only mistake was mouthin' off to the boss," Silas said. A sneer consuming his ugly face.

"Madame, I won't ask again. Will you come with us?"

"Stay out of this," she said to me in a low voice over her shoulder. Without waiting for a response, her foot lashed out and struck Granville squarely in the crotch. The knife clattered to the floor as he grasped himself, groaning. She executed a right turn, driving her fist into Silas's gut, dropping him like an ox at the slaughterhouse.

Laurel Anne swung her club at Victoria's back, but she danced aside. Swift as forge hammer, she snatched a mug off the trappers' table and slammed it into the woman's head. She joined his friends on the floor.

"Hey, that was my ale!" the trapper complained.

Victoria flipped a silver coin onto the table. "Next round's on me."

She swept out of the pub and I followed. As my first "official" mission since Roland's death, I'd wanted something easy. How hard could killing a rogue bear be?

Obviously, a lot harder than I expected.

7

Outside the wind had picked up, sending sheets of dirt and debris down the street in waves. Victoria snapped her goggles and respirator into place. "Lots of wind and not a lot of rain in Stillhold. Pays to be prepared."

I tied a cloth across my face before following my fellow Watcher down the street. The dust, undeterred by my makeshift mask, found its way into my lungs, making me cough. The impending storm whipped the town like a mule driver in a hurry to get home. My eyes fought to clear themselves of the grit. Victoria's stride increased as she turned down a small alley I'd have missed.

For the next half hour, we stalked between buildings, dodging the worst of the dust storm, hiding in the dark recesses until Victoria was confident we weren't being followed. "Can't be too careful, " she said. "Spencer's goons are getting more determined by the day. I'll have to do something about him sooner or later, though I might need a bit of help."

We continued on. Wyndham slid between rancid piles of

trash, which made the stinging wind a pleasure. I held my breath as I navigated the lumps of unidentifiable debris. The light dimmed as we pushed deeper between two warehouses. Victoria stopped and worked a concealed lever to open a hidden door.

Inside, alarium lights dotted the white walls of the laboratory. Victoria's workspace was controlled chaos, with glassware and other instruments I didn't recognize stacked all over wooden benches and tables. She hung her long coat, goggles, and respirator on the wall before tying on a leather apron similar to mine for the forge.

She turned to face me, an annoyed look on her long, thin face. She must be a few years older than I, maybe thirty, but her experience placed her far above me. "Do you know how stupid it is to mention the Watchers in a place like the Broken Spoke? If you want to return to Treetop, you need to think first and talk after."

My cheeks heated as I was scolded like a child, but if the shoe fit, you nailed it in place. "I guess I was surprised."

She looked down at her body and leapt back as if startled. "Oh my, I'm a woman," she exclaimed in a mocking tone. Her eyes locked on mine. "Listen, junior--"

"Quinn."

"I don't care if you're Everard. Have you never seen a woman before or did you think the Watchers was a boy's club?" Her eyes blazed like a stoked fire and I was the iron she was about to liquify.

My head dropped, breaking her glare. "I've only met Cian, Everard, and Roland."

"Well, Roland should have…" Her voice trailed off and she tapped her chin as she considered me. "Roland died before he'd fully trained you, didn't he?"

"Yes, ma'am."

"Call me Victoria. or Mistress Wyndham, if you're feeling

formal." After another excruciating minute, she said, "You mentioned you needed me to examine a substance you found?"

"Yes, ma'am, err, Victoria." I fumbled in my sack for the blue liquid, which I unpacked carefully out of its box. It had survived the trip intact, which I couldn't say about my nerves. I held up the stoppered syringe.

"Where in the world did you get that?"

"From an armored bear that killed a lot of people."

"I need to hear this story." Victoria took the syringe from me, holding it up to the light. She motioned me to sit on the stool across from her and we both sat. "Let me hear your story, Quinn."

I told her about Cian and I fighting the bear before we were forced to kill it. She murmured her approval. I described the process I'd used to examine the device and how I thought the mechanism worked.

"What do you think is behind the attacks?" she asked. "What do the three towns have in common?"

"Nothing as far as I can see," I said, absently scratching the spot where my mechanical arm met skin.

She noticed, quirking an eyebrow.

I stopped scratching and settled my hands. "Usorin tried to kill my mentor and took my arm instead. Roland found me and, once I was healed, brought me into the Watch. We built a replacement arm. I modified the design to mimic the magus devices for combat."

Victoria nodded, her lips pursed. "Roland was a good man and a great Watcher."

"Yeah," I said glumly. "I've got big shoes to fill."

"So did Roland," she said with a chuckle. "We all have our strengths and weaknesses. You'll learn."

"And if I don't?"

She cocked her head, a strange expression on her face.

"Then you'll die, I assume. Now, let's take a look at the present you brought me."

I stood up, startled at the abrupt change of subject. Victoria was a unique person to be sure.

She unstoppered the syringe, emptying the contents into a glass tube on her workbench. "I'll need a day or so to ascertain the nature of this elixir. I'll call on you at the Broken Spoke when I know more."

"What do you think it is?"

She shook her head, "If I knew that already, I wouldn't need a day to research, would I?"

"True."

She smirked at me, a twinkle in her eye. "Do you know what happened when the red ship crashed into the blue ship?"

"No."

"They were marooned." She burst into laughter. I left, shaking my head the whole way.

✦

I backtracked to the main street of Stillhold. The winds hadn't stopped, but they weren't trying to knock me over as I walked, either. The sun was beginning to set in the west. I shielded my eyes from the worst of the dirt and wandered around until I found the general store I'd seen earlier. If I was staying in Stillhold, I needed goggles and a respirator. I pushed my way against the wind until I reached the heavy wooden door and, with an effort, wedged it open enough to slip inside.

"Don't let the door--"

Boom! The door slammed behind me, the force of the wind driving it into the frame hard enough to shake the floor. Luckily the frame held under the assault.

"Slam," finished the woman behind the counter. She wore a plaid shawl draped around her shoulders over a dark dress with a long white apron. "Did your ma not teach you about slammin' doors?"

"No, ma'am," I stuttered. "She died when I was young. I didn't mean to let the door slam."

The woman scowled a bit before relaxing. Strands of dark hair snuck out from under her bonnet. Her goggles and a respirator hung around her neck. "Well, can't be blamin' you if' in you weren't taught. What can I do ya fer?"

Supplies of all types populated the store's shelves. The store displayed blankets, bags of oats and flour, cans of oil, along with an assortment of farming supplies and tools. Metal mining lanterns, block and tackle, and other gear hung from the rafters. A curtain covered an exit that led to the rear of the building. Behind the counter were various canned goods along with an assortment of goggles and respirators.

"I'd like to buy a pair of goggles and a respirator," I said, approaching the counter. An ancient mechanical cash register was positioned behind a set of glass jars filled with candy.

She gave me an appraising look before retrieving a dull grey set of goggles and a respirator from the shelf behind the register. I picked the goggles up. Tin. If I put any pressure on them, they'd dent. The respirator was even more flimsy, without mesh or weave to keep the dirt out.

"Seriously?" I asked, trying to keep the irritation out of my voice. My Watcher mask would be far more effective, but a Watcher couldn't exactly walk around town without causing a ruckus. When there was an emergency everyone was glad to see the Watchers, the rest of the time we were viewed with suspicion if not outright hostility.

She shrugged. "You don't look like you've got a silver to your name, let alone the three those cost."

"Three silvers? These are tin. The lens will crack in a stiff wind, and without a filter, I'd choke on the dirt."

She grunted, putting the tin pieces back. The next set appeared no better and I had no patience to spend all day doing this.

"Give me the brass fitted ones on the top shelf."

"Those are two gold. I'll need to see your coin." Her eyes narrowed like a street fighter watching their opponent.

I held up my hands. "You're wasting my time, I'll do without." I turned on my heel and headed toward the door.

I heard her sigh. "One gold for the set?" The note of uncertainty rang out in her words.

"Let me see them." I returned to the counter as she stepped on a short stool and pulled them down. She wiped them on her apron before handing them over.

The goggles had real glass lenses and mechanical fittings so they could be replaced if damaged. The sides contained a small set of grates to allow moisture to escape without allowing in dirt, smoke, or anything else. The respirator held a bag of charcoal that smelled slightly sulfuric. It would neutralize odors and gas. Overkill for what I needed, but I'd quenched my iron so now I was stuck paying for it. "These are better quality, but still not worth a gold."

She cast an appraising glance at me. "How do you know?"

I explained the craftsmanship of the piece and pointed out the benefits of such a setup. She nodded along as I spoke, interrupting to ask a couple of questions. I was in my element, discussing metallurgy, design, and fabrication.

"Are you a tinker?" she asked suddenly, cutting off my lecture on the benefits of using brass instead of bronze.

I shook my head. "No, I was a blacksmith, until my mentor died."

She chewed her lip for a second. "I'll give 'em to you fer

half a gold if you'll fix my register. Hasn't worked for a spell and I can't get it open."

"Deal. I'm Randolph." I said, supplying the alias I'd taken for this mission. I reached out my hand and she took it with a firm shake.

"Millicent Habsburg. I appreciate you fixin' this old hunk of junk."

She stepped aside to let me see the register, if you could call it that. It looked like a cross between a metal box and a steam engine. Pistons, gears, and rivets were on every available surface. A glass window showed a "No Sale" chit displayed within. Millicent peered over my shoulder as I pulled out my traveling kit.

She whistled softly as I unrolled the oilskin, displaying my tools. "You must be a tinker, carryin' stuff like that."

Having a quality set of tools had come in handy more times than I cared to remember. When you depended on a mechanical arm, being able to effect repairs was a necessity. "I trained as an artificer when I was younger. You never know when you'll need to fix a mudstone lamp or a register."

"Lucky for me, then. Dang thing's been locked up for months." She pulled a stool over and perched on it, straightening her white apron over her knees.

I checked the drawer mechanism. The locking pin was engaged, but not jammed. The easy fix would be to depress the lock and open the drawer, but that wouldn't prevent the issue from recurring. Plus the return key was frozen in place, which was strange because it wasn't in disrepair. I finished my inspection of the device and nothing else appeared out of order.

"Can ya fix'er?" Millicent asked, doubt heavy in her tone.

"Probably." I rounded the counter, looking for the machine's internal access panel. The candy jars blocked my view of the register's rear plate.

"You break even one of those and I'll tan your hide."

I nodded, carefully setting the jars off to the side. From the back of the register, two small pipes ran down through the counter. "Where do these pipes lead?"

She shrugged. "Don't know. Mr. Habsburg always took care of the store."

"I'm sorry for your loss."

She barked a laugh. "Loss? He's a drunk and ran off on some damn trading adventure. Left me with nothin' but this shop and a lot of debt. Best thing ever happened was him leavin'."

Well, at least I hadn't put the wrong shoe on the horse. "Mind if I look around?"

She clenched her hands together, but said, "Suit yourself."

I searched the room, trying not to trip over the piles of supplies. Millicent had quite the selection for being so far away from a large city. After a few minutes, I found a half door in the wall behind a decent quality mechanical harvester the size of a small donkey. The door revealed an old generator.

This was an old version of a generator, but instead of alarium, it ran off mudstone that didn't last very long. It wasn't running. I primed the pump, but nothing happened. After a couple of minutes, I found the compartment that held the power source. I unscrewed the couplings and removed the top. The chamber held nothing but faint brown dust. It had simply run out of fuel.

I straightened and returned. "Mrs. Habsburg, do you have any mudstone on hand?"

Her eyes narrowed, but she nodded. She took down a tin labeled mudstone from the shelving behind the register and produced a sizable chunk of the semi-precious stone. I placed it in the chamber, reassembled the housings, primed the pump, and started it up. Lights flicked on overhead and the register banged open with a clang. Coins scattered across the floor, all of them gold.

That was when I noticed Millicent pointing a small crossbow at me.

I'd fallen from the tongs into the fire.

8

The curtain at the back of the store swished open, and Granville from the Broken Spoke, flanked by Silas and Laurel Anne, sauntered out. Granville pulled an older woman behind him. Her hands were tied before her and a gag was shoved in her mouth. Tears rolled down her plump cheeks.

"Mrs. Habsburg, are you all right?" I asked gently as I sized up the situation. The crossbow was the biggest threat, but only until the woman fired it. I doubted she could reload it, given the pull of the bow. I was more concerned about the bruised, battered, and probably resentful men holding the real Millicent Habsburg.

Case in point, Granville pulled her in front of him and placed a long hunting knife near her throat. Since I hadn't brought my weapons, I'd have to rely on other skills. Roland had trained me in hand-to-hand combat, and it was four on one.

"Of course, she's all right, lad," Granville said, though I noticed he stood a bit gingerly. "Imagine you just strollin' on in here when we spent the day lookin' fer ya. Unless you want the old woman to get sliced up, you'll be taking us to see Lady Yorke once we're done here. Do that, and we'll let you go. Decide to be a hero and you'll bleed. Either way, you'll take us to her. Understand?"

I nodded, keeping my eyes on the floor, acting like a good mouse. I needed to get within arm's reach of the knife. Then the real fight would begin. "I can take you to her, but only if you release Mrs. Habsburg."

The leader waved the knife in my direction. "See, the lad is reasonable and we've no gripe with him." He pushed the old woman to the side, where Silas caught her. He had a small club, not a knife, making my job easier. "Edwina, gather up the coin our young friend was nice enough to free up for us."

Millicent, trying to talk through her gag, protested the robbery I'd facilitated. Granville raised his baton to strike her.

Guilt at being fooled so easily galled me. "Leave the coin. She's done nothing to hurt you."

Granville brandished the knife, gesturing at me to emphasize his point. "You're a stranger here, lad. This woman has stolen from the poor people of Stillhold as if she'd put a knife to their throats herself. Ask her how many farms died after the river broke?"

"What do you mean the river broke?"

He smiled at me like I was an ignorant child. "Boy, them wizards got into a fight upstream. When all was said and done, the river stopped flowing past Stillhold and flooded out the down country."

This must be what the bartender was talking about. Was Everard involved? He had to be. The magus' all used the alarium powered sleeves to effect their "magic" and there wasn't enough power in them to divert a river. "How does that make it Mrs. Habsberg's fault?"

"Did she offer equipment to drill wells to irrigate? No, she just let them starve or bought up their lands and offered to rent the land back to the farmers with a well—at a ridiculous price. Does that sound like a saint?"

"Sounds like a business. How many debts did your boss excuse during the hard times? I would guess zero." His cheeks flushed. Behind me Edwina tossed the previously trapped coins into a burlap bag, giggling the whole time.

"And why should he? Master Spencer lends to those in need, but he expects his money returned to him. The Lady Yorke owes him a right sum, and I'm going to make sure he gets it. Now let's finish this. Master Spencer is a man of little patience."

I nodded. The crossbow rested on the counter next to Edwina. She'd lost her focus while loading up the coins. "Why are these all covered in grease?" Edwina complained. She cleaned one-off with the hem of her dress. "I told you Lemuel said there was a fortune stuck in here and I was the only one smart enough to figure it out."

Granville rounded on her. "That coin is for Master Spencer, not a trollop like you, Edwina. Don't you go forget-tin' it."

I doubted I'd get a better chance. I dove at Granville. He twisted at the last second, my punch landing on his shoulder instead of his jaw. He bellowed in pain as my metal fist struck.

Edwina's burlap bag crashed to the floor with the jingle of spilling coins. She grabbed the crossbow and fired without aiming. The shot ricocheted off my arm and pierced the woman's chest, dropping her.

"Laurel Anne!" she cried, running to the fallen woman.

Silas charged at me faster than I'd predicted given the number of things in the way. His baton struck me across the face, hard enough to knock me back from him and his weapon. He advanced, launching another blow at my head. The fight would have been over except my foot caught on a bag of flour and I crashed to the floor, avoiding the finishing blow.

"Don't kill him," Granville yelled over Edwina's anguished screams. "We need him to find the woman."

I don't think the man listened. He swung overhanded at me. Using my metal arm as a shield, I blocked the attack. With a swift kick, I struck his knee, buckling the leg. Baton and man alike fell to the ground.

In hopes of a quick knockout, I threw a punch at his head. He rolled aside, pulling a knife from his boot before he climbed to his feet.

"Now we'll see how well you bleed," Silas said between gritted teeth.

The knife flashed, and a rent appeared in my sleeve, revealing the bronze metal underneath. "What kind of demon be you?"

"Not a demon, just an injured man."

Silas lunged, the knife held like a spear. I caught the blade in my metal hand and snapped it clean off. While he stared at his broken weapon, I punched him in the jaw, dropping him like a bad habit.

Before I could reach her, Granville grabbed Millicent and held his knife in his left hand while his right hung uselessly at his side from the earlier punch. "I'll kill her if you come any closer, stranger."

I had been taken advantage of and underestimated and my patience had run out. It was time to put an end to this. "Let her go and you can walk out of here."

He shook his head, anguish and fear reflected in his eyes. "I don't bring in Lady Yorke, I won't live to see tomorrow, lad. Master Spencer doesn't brook well with failure."

Which meant he had nothing left to lose. Before I could

do anything, Millicent Habsburg nodded forward as if she would faint.

With a flick of my wrist, I sent the broken blade sailing over Granville's head.

He laughed when it missed, but it wasn't long-lasting. The knife sliced through the thin cord holding a mining lantern in place. He looked up in time for the lantern to crash into his face. When he fell to the floor with a hiss of pain, Mrs. Habsburg stumbled free.

I pulled my belt knife and cut Millicent's bonds. She pulled the gag from her mouth and proceeded to kick the man who'd threatened her life. I led her behind the counter, pushing the crossbow out of the way, and settled her onto a stool. "Did they hurt you?"

"No, son. Thank ye for saving me. My husband's been gone for a few years. I'm glad you got the register opened. That money was for me to run the place, but the register stopped working right after he left. Let me reward you for saving me."

I smiled at her. "I'm going to finish this." Edwina sobbed on the floor next to Laurel Anne's body. The quill had pierced her heart from the looks of it. I knelt next to her. "How much does Lady Yorke owe Master Spencer?"

She flinched away from my touch. "Granville would know." She gestured toward where the leader lay on the floor clutching his bloodied face. I left her in her misery and pulled Granville to his feet. "How much does Lady Yorke owe?"

Blood spattered me as he slurred out the answer. "Twelve gold, but Spencer wants her more than the coin."

"Gold will have to do." I dragged him behind me. "Mrs. Habsburg, I hate to impose..."

She held out a handful of gold coins. "There are fifteen there. Spencer is a hard man, so be careful."

"I will. Thank you." The coins were slick with oil, not grease. I looked to her for an explanation.

"I tried to oil the lock, thinking it was stuck. I guess I used too much."

I chuckled. "Well, these won't stick to anything now. I'll pay you back as soon as I can."

She shook her head and handed me the brass goggles and respirator. "You'll need these. The least I can do is help you get your friend out of debt."

I nodded, knowing I was done with the easy part of my day. As a Watcher, I should have taken Edwina into custody for murder. Unfortunately, they'd seen my face and I couldn't risk revealing I was a Watcher. It would be up to "Randolph", not Watcher Quinn to set this straight.

It was time to walk into the lion's den and face down the king.

9

I half dragged, half carried Granville through the maelstrom of the oncoming storm, thankful for the goggles and respirator Mrs. Habsburg had given me. Granville stumbled and cursed as I propelled him into the teeth of the wind. I may have 'forgotten' his gear back at the shop. No skin off my nose, but his nose was in rough shape at this point.

After a few minutes, we reached a wooden building sporting a faded sign proclaiming it the Gilded Lily. I pushed our way through the heavy wooden door into the main room of the brothel. A few girls stared at us, glassy-eyed, as I shoved Granville down on the floor in front of me. He squawked, landing with a thud. I'd have dragged his accomplices with us, but they were taking Laurel Anne to the morgue.

The room was well appointed with brass fixtures and mirrors covering the walls. Stairs led up to a walkway that wrapped around the main room. Glass chandeliers hung low, casting a soft light that made the room feel richer than the furnishings alone ever could. Small tables dotted the area before the mammoth bar which was made of polished brass, glass, and a series of gears across the front. What happened when the gears turned? My professional curiosity would have to wait.

A large woman in a silk robe and elaborate hairdo strolled across the room toward us. Her gaze fixed on Granville. "You ain't lookin' so hot, honey."

Granville lifted his head. "Mama Rosalie, I ain't feelin' so good." His words were muffled by his broken nose.

Rosalie's gaze meandered over me. I didn't take off the goggles but slipped the respirator down so I could speak.

"You here on business or pleasure, sweetheart?" she asked pointedly. "Maybe a bit of both?"

I tamped down on the flush that tried to color my cheeks. "Business, ma'am. I need to speak to Master Spencer."

"Such a shame. Well, follow me." When I stopped to grab Granville, she added, "My boys will take care of the trash."

Granville whimpered but didn't say anything. I followed Rosalie past the opulent bar and through a doorway into a large office. The walls were paneled in a dark wood, broken only by a large stone fireplace that contained a roaring fire. A thick rug covered the floor in front of the mahogany desk with two alarium lamps. Master Spencer must be worth a small fortune.

A man leaned back in his chair, puffing on a cigar. A glass of amber liquid rested in front of him. He was a larger man, not fat, but sturdily built, like one of the haulers I'd known as a boy. His hairline receded from an oversized nose that ended in a vicious hook.

When he spoke, it was in a deep, booming voice. "Allow me to introduce myself. I'm Master Spencer, owner of the Guilded Lilly. And you are?"

I ignored the question. "I've come to settle up Lady Yorke's debt to you."

"So, you must be the companion of Lady Yorke I've heard about. Why have you abused my men and come here? Mayhap you wish to die?"

I pulled twelve gold coins from the pouch on my belt and tossed them on the desk. "There's your coin. You and Lady Yorke are square, as I see it."

Spencer laughed as he raked his hands through the scattered coins. He examined his oily fingers before cleaning them on his handkerchief. "Boy, you come into my place of business and declare a debt been paid? That's not how these things work. Lady Yorke owes me twelve gold and a favor. You can't repay that."

Rosalie simpered like a schoolgirl at the implications. I glared at her, though I doubt she could tell with my goggles on.

I was about to speak when the door opened and Watcher Wyndham herself strode in. Her apron had been replaced by a sturdy leather coat, leather gauntlets, and a large revolver. "Spencer, our game has been fun, but as usual, you've gone too far."

Another bout of laughter erupted from the big man. "Ah, my Lady Yorke. To what do I owe the honor of your visit?"

I wasn't sure what her game was, but I was fascinated by how she spoke to Master Spencer.

Victoria's eyes burned like a hot and uncontrollable coal ash fire. "How dare you sic your mutts on the Widow Habsburg? I knew you had few morals, but this is beyond reproach."

Spencer's fist struck the top of his desk, jangling the coins and threatening to topple his drink. "It is you that goes too far, Lady Yorke. I lent you coin in good faith and this is how you repay me?"

The fire in her eyes went out like a bucket of water had doused it. "You're right. Instead, I will offer you a gift." She pulled a small glass vial from the inner pocket of her coat. It held a green liquid that sparkled in the light cast from the alarium lamps. "I bestow upon thee the elixir of life."

"What foolery is this?" Spencer demanded, but his eyes clung to the vial in her fingertips. "Even with your alchemical skills, there is no such thing."

Victoria cocked her head, considering his words. "True for most, but this truly is life for you, Spencer." She spun the vial neatly in her fingers. "Master Randolph paid my debt. Did you touch the coins?"

Spencer's face grew concerned as he held up his hands, noticing the residue from the oily gold. "Why?"

Victoria must have spoken with Mrs. Habsburg before following me here.

Wyndham smiled brightly. "Contact poison, I'm afraid, and this is the antidote. Well, at least the first one."

"First one?" Rosalie's eyes widened like she'd touched a hot iron.

"Rosalie's got the picture. The poison will stay in your system. Every week, I'll leave a vial of the antidote with Widow Habsburg. I'll leave it up to her if she'd like to deliver it. Vex the poor woman, and your life will be over. Do we understand each other?"

Spencer's gaze went from the vial to Wyndham to me. His eyes lit up as he said, "What about your man there? He touched the coins. You're bluffing."

I held up my hand, covered in a leather glove. "I took precautions."

Spencer's shoulders slumped in defeat. "Name your terms."

"You may keep the coin, though you may want to wash them. As you correctly stated, I did borrow it from you and I have returned it with the interest as agreed."

Spencer didn't say anything so Victoria continued. "Second, if your men come after me or the Widow, your supply of antidote will cease and you will die a horrible, excruciatingly painful death."

"Anything else?" Spencer mumbled as he placed his elbows heavily on his desk.

"No." Victoria slid the vial across the desk to Spencer, who uncorked it and drank it greedily.

Spencer leaned back into his chair. "We're done here. Get out of my office."

Rosalie approached, shooing us. I stepped toward the door, but Victoria held her ground.

Wyndham's voice was light and airy as she asked, "Spencer, what kind of tea is hard to swallow?"

His face darkened. "I have no time for your foolishness. Get out."

Victoria smiled sweetly. "Reali-ty." With that, she pivoted on her heel and strode from the room.

The woman could definitely make an exit.

10

Victoria escorted me back to the Broken Spoke and asked me to stay out of trouble. I thought about arguing with her, but given the day I'd had, I just agreed and ate an early dinner in my room. I spent the evening maintaining my arm, though one-handed was always a challenge.

The next morning, I was eating breakfast in the common room of the Broken Spoke when Victoria sauntered through the front door. She wore a long, dark coat over a peacock green shirt and grey pants. She slid her goggles and respirator down as she approached my table and took a seat across from me.

"Good morn, Randolph." Her bloodshot eyes hinted at a lack of sleep.

"Good morning, Lady Yorke." I set my bowl aside and wiped my hands on the cloth napkin. "Did you find out about the package I left with you?"

She smirked. "Why, yes, I have. If you're done with your breakfast, there are things we need to discuss."

No jokes or wordplay. Worry seeped up my back into my

brain. I dropped a couple of coppers on the table and adjusted my goggles and respirator as she opened the door. While the storm wasn't as intense as the previous days, it was still enough for me to be thankful for them.

Wyndham took a different route to the laboratory, stopping three times to ensure we weren't followed. I didn't say anything, and given the whistling of the wind, conversations were best held indoors. After she was assured we were alone, we entered her hideout.

Her coat and goggles were hung on a hook. I pulled mine off as well, setting them on a small table near the door. A gunpowder revolver sat on the workbench near the door. "Expecting trouble?"

Victoria perched on a stool. "Quinn, tell me how you got this again?"

I repeated the story about the bear Cian and I had defeated outside of Lapis. This time she fired off questions, picking at details as if looking for the hidden seed of truth.

"I am forced to say I believe you, but what you've brought me is highly troubling, to say the least." She grabbed a piece of parchment and handed it to me "I've run a series of tests and have reverified the results to eliminate any false positives or testing errors."

I waited as she collected her thoughts. Concern etched her face like the design on an artificer's plate. After a moment I prompted her. "And?"

"Sorry, lack of sleep is making me a bit foggy." She adjusted her leather apron. "The fluid in the vial is benzodiazepine mixed with a cyclopyrrolone."

As an artificer, I knew my fair share of large words, but Victoria may as well have been speaking Nornish. "I don't know what any of that means."

"I didn't think you would," Victoria said as she set the paper back down on the workbench. "Both are strong drugs, used to treat patients in asylums. They make the patients more pliable, open to suggestion. Mixed, they form a drug that borders on hypnotic. If the device on the animal's back was pumping this into its system, someone could easily control the poor thing's mind to force it to follow simple commands."

I pulled the pouch off my belt and removed the mechanical piece I'd taken from the bear. I handed it to Victoria, who studied it carefully before returning it to me.

"What is it?" she asked.

I shook my head. "It is probably how the bear was controlled. If no one was nearby to direct it, then this instrument must be how they forced the bear to attack the villagers."

"Makes sense," She pushed her long black ponytail over her shoulder. "The real question is why attack the villages in the first place?"

I'd been wondering the same thing. None of the towns were overly wealthy, nor traded in products that were scarce. No large merchant routes ran through them. The magi rulers weren't known for atrocities or mismanaging their holdings. In fact, Nigel of House Hawk had a reputation as a bit of a philanthropist, giving to the people of Aldon far more than Usorin had ever given Terralon.

"I've been over the attacks in my head, but there are no common denominators. If it was revenge, why attack three towns? None of the towns hold strategic or political value. I need to find out who is behind this."

Victoria nodded her agreement. "It is a sticky situation. With Aurelia Salwey's death in the first bear attack, there isn't a Watcher in Aldon. I guess that's where you come in."

"Then why didn't Cian handle the latest attack? Aldon is on the other end of the country from me." Why I'd been sent to deal with this situation perplexed me since I was only responsible for Terralon. And if I recalled correctly, Roland had traveled all over the country. "I thought the Watchers served Astaria as a whole?"

Victoria sighed. The dark rings under her eyes told the story of how exhausted she was. "Those would be questions for Everard, but my guess is you have a skill he needed. Each of us has abilities that we use in the defense of Astaria. The trick is to use your specific skills to carry out the mission of protecting the Astarian people. You couldn't use alchemey to solve a problem any more than I could forge a solution. You have to approach things from your point of view, not someone else's."

What had Everard expected I could do more than an experienced Watch member? I definitely would be discussing this further with him at his earliest convenience. "I appreciate the information, both on the fluid and on the Watchers. I doubt I'll ever understand all of this."

She laughed. "You will, Quinn. It's only been six months. Most of us apprentice for years before we move to our own region. Time is the coin of our trade."

My mentor had been killed before I'd had much training. Sometimes iron breaks and ends up in the scrap pile. That doesn't stop you from forging a new piece. "Speaking of coins, how long until Spencer realizes you didn't poison him?"

She cocked her head. "Who says I didn't poison him?"

"Well, the coins were coated in oil, not poison, and you gave him the antidote."

She smiled, mischief dancing in her brown eyes. "Did I now? How do you know it was the antidote?"

"You told him it was."

"I did," she said, shrugging her shoulders, her hands spread out in front of her. "And of course, a lady would never lie."

After a moment, I realized what she'd done. "The vial was the poison."

She clapped her approval. "Spencer is a rabid animal, but if I remove him, someone worse might take over. By poisoning him, I can control him and keep him from killing more innocent people. This is what I mean by using your skills to solve problems. Dead, he's no good to me, but poisoned he'll do as I say or he will be gone."

Ruthless but practical. "Thank you, Victoria. Today has been very educational."

"A child comes home from school and is asked, 'What did you learn today?'" Victoria said as I snapped my goggles back into place.

"And the child says?"

"Not enough, I have to go back tomorrow."

I groaned and headed out the door into the wind.

The words rang true, though. I'd have to keep learning tomorrow if I wanted to find the person responsible for the bear attack.

11

I caught the airship back to Bradenbridge, staying overnight at the Brass Gear before riding the two days to Treetop. On my way out of Bradenbridge, I stopped to buy some supplies I'd need. No sense going home empty-handed.

The puzzle of the bear, the drug, and the mysterious magic device ran circles in my brain as I steered the cart along the path I'd come to know quite well. The answer was in front of me; I just couldn't see it. Victoria had said to use my talents to solve issues, but blacksmithing or artificing didn't get me any closer to catching the person responsible for the attacks. At least as far as I could see.

I stepped off the lift contemplating my dilemma. No Jabber. He always waited at the door for my return. "Jabber?" I said, setting down the provisions and entering into the living area. The door to the workshop stood open with no signs of Jabber or anyone else. The last time I'd returned to find Treetop empty, I discovered the corpse of my mentor. A mix of fear and energy throbbed through my body as I turned the corner that led to the sleeping areas and the kitchen.

"Quinn," Everard yelped as he jumped back. The stew in a wooden bowl slopped over his hands as he adjusted his grip. Jabber followed behind the Arch Magus with a small cask of ale. "Good to see you, Master Quinn, but I hadn't expected you until tomorrow."

"What are you doing here?" I asked, my voice trembling from the shock of seeing another person in my home. Jabber was part of Treetop, but Everard was an unexpected guest.

"Let me put this down before I spill it all." He stepped past me, heading for the long table in the living area.

Jabber approached me. "The Arch Magus is authorized to enter Treetop," the automaton said, his voice neutral as ever. "Is that not correct?"

I shook my head in disbelief. Why would Everard be here? "He's allowed to enter, just wasn't expecting anyone else. Can you put the provisions away while I talk with Everard? I'll take the ale."

"Of course," Jabber said with a slight bow. He handed me the cask and the cup. I needed to figure out how to adjust him to be a bit less formal, but that would have to wait. I walked down the hall and retrieved a second mug.

Everard sat at the table eating the stew. I took the stool across from him, poured us each a mug of ale, and waited for him to explain why he was at Treetop.

He sipped at the ale and nodded approvingly. "Good beer. You asked why I've come to visit, as it were," he said in a joking tone. "Two reasons, really. Cian told me about the incident in Aldon, and you need to practice your magic, so I am here to teach you."

I groaned inside. Everard had been Arch Magus since before I was born. Unlike Roland's patient lessons, Evarard's idea of teaching was constant repetition until it worked or you fell over from exhaustion. Not exactly the best learning environment. It might be better to bang my head against the table until I got the hang of magic.

Everard held up a hand. "I realize we've been less than successful in our other training sessions, but I've got a few ideas. First off, tell me what you've found so far about the bear."

I took a swing from my mug, collecting my thoughts. I had to agree, it was a good beer. "Where do you want me to begin?"

"From where you encountered the bear."

I launched into the story, going over the fight and how pulling the box free had stopped the rampage and killed the bear in the process. I shared the information Victoria had given me and the conclusions I'd had that the device was being used to control the bear from a distance. He sipped at his beer while I spoke, stopping me to ask questions.

He refilled both our beers when I came to the end. "Can I see the device?"

I fished it out of my pouch and handed it over. He studied the runes and inscriptions carefully, before placing it on the table. He muttered a few words as he made a series of gestures over the device.

Nothing happened for a few moments until a raspy male voice emanated from the air above the small box. "Kill the magus and bring me..."

The voice dwindled to nothing.

"Interesting," Everard said. A single bead of sweat rolled down his cheek. "Not much to go on, but we know it's a male who was directing the bear. The real question is why concentrate on you when Cian was the greater threat?"

I started to agree, but then remembered. "Maybe, but one of the Aldon magus was onsite. He threw lightning at the beast before it killed him and tried to drag his body away. The townsfolk threatened and the bear attacked them."

"Why would a bear drag off one corpse after killing so many?" Everard asked.

I couldn't answer that question. Each piece of information held nothing in common with the rest. I had a bench full of parts and no plan to show me what to build. I took another drink and waited for Everard to say something.

"I'll sleep on it and maybe in the morning I'll have a better idea of what to do next," Everard said.

"Next?"

Everard scoffed. "Come now, Quinn. You can't believe someone who went to all that trouble to kill a bunch of villagers would stop that easily, did you?"

The Arch Magus was right. It was only a matter of time before another bear, or something worse, showed up. But when and where…and why? "What do they have to gain from killing villagers?"

"Well that certainly is a question we'd like to answer, but we'll need to keep searching until we find it." He clapped his hands as he rose. "Now, let's try a couple of simple spells to warm up."

I forced myself to stand. Everard straightened and breathed deeply which I mimicked. He paced me through the exercises his master had used to teach him about magic. In my observations, magic was altering energy to accomplish your goal. What deep breathing and arm-waving had to do with it, I didn't know, but I was game to try anything at this point. At least he was trying something different than the last set of lessons.

"Now," Everard said when I was sufficiently warmed up. "Start with Lenthal um Tral. It will levitate an object. I tried magic too complex last time, so this is as simple as it gets."

"Lenthal um Tral," I said, envisioning my mug rising off the table. Nothing happened.

"Quinn, you need to use gestures to unlock the magic. Watch." He crossed his wrists, hooking his thumbs together so they looked like a bird. He spoke the words as he curled his fingers, and his mug rose smoothly into the air. As he uncurled his fingers the mug settled back to the wooden table. "Now you try."

I repeated his steps as exactly as I could and still, nothing happened. "Maybe my metal arm interferes with the magic."

Everard shook his head. "Try it again, but make sure your thumbs are interlocked." I did and still no results. For over an hour I tried to float the mug, but voice inflection, finger position, and everything else yielded nothing but frustration.

"You have to believe it will work, Quinn. You must be doubting the magic or yourself. I can't think of anything else that would be stopping you."

"Maybe it's his teacher," a soft voice said from behind me. I pivoted to see a woman in a blue robe, silver runes surrounding the cowl and wrists. She pushed back her hood, exposing deep golden skin, lavender eyes, and features so delicate they could have been made of glass. Long black hair draped behind her.

Everard knelt on one knee and I followed suit. "My lady Maelyrra. To what do we owe the honor of your visit?"

"You are ruining my mage, Everard, and I want you to stop."

I remained on my knees, head bowed, wondering what to do. The Lady Maelyrra had bestowed my magic upon me to defend Astaria from our common foes. I still had no idea which dimension she came from or why she had chosen me to aid Everard with true magic. The nobles used devices such as my shield generator to mimic magical abilities, but if I could ever get my powers to work I would be far more effective.

"Stand up, Quinn. I would converse with you."

Thunderstruck, I stood. What was so important to risk the danger of crossing over to our dimension? She could have summoned me instead.

"Everard, leave us." She dismissed the Arch Magus with a wave. "I have need to speak with Quinn, alone." The emphasis on the word "alone" would have pierced even the dimmest of listeners. Everard, being far more intelligent, huffed once, bowed to Maelyrra, and proceeded to leave the room.

"Lady Maelyrra, how can I be of service?"

She floated just off the floor, the hem of her blue robe

billowing slightly as if a gentle breeze stirred it. "Your mastery of the magical arts has not progressed beyond rudimentary. I came to find out why, but I would like to know your thoughts on the matter."

A headache crept up my neck as my heart pounded. Would she take away the magic if I didn't master it? I felt like a child who'd been gifted a wonderful machine with nothing to tell them what it did or how to operate it. All of the parts were on the table before me, but there was no way for me to make them work. Honestly, I'd stopped trying out of frustration. I sighed. "I have done everything the Arch Magus has demonstrated and nothing works. He's left me notes and practicums, and I can barely light a candle with my magic. I feel like I have failed you."

Maelyrra nodded, her eyes full of warmth and interest. "Let me ask you a question. Would you put a horseshoe on a cow?"

My spinning thoughts halted at the unexpected question. The shock must have shown on my face for a gentle smile graced her lips. "No, of course not."

"Why?"

"Horses and cows have very different hooves. Even if the shoe fit, hammering the nails in would hurt the cow. It would be cruel to the animal."

"Exactly. So why would you learn magic the same way Everard did?"

"I..." Words fled as my brain failed to produce a reason. I floundered and finally spit out, "Because he learned it that way and that is how magic works."

Her eyes glittered in the afternoon sun that streamed in the windows. "Are all blacksmiths trained the same?"

I shook my head. "No, my lady. Some take to it quicker or have an eye for how the metal moves under the hammer. You adjust the training to suit the student."

"Agreed. So again, why learn magic the way Everard did? It is possible an off-handed solution would be more effective." Her serene expression informed me she wasn't upset or angry at all.

Why was I learning Everard's way? Everard's magic was strong and had saved lives, thwarted Norn and Candalarian attacks, and kept the Astarian magi in check. Not to mention there weren't any other true magi in Astaria. In the absence of another source, you returned to the fire you had.

Except…I never had been willing to sacrifice the quality of my work because of limitations. I would build a bigger forge bed or add mudstone to increase the temperature if that was what it took. I wouldn't settle for the fire I was given. Why should I do it with magic, when I didn't do it with the rest of my life? My master blacksmith had always told me a true artisan had to go his own way, not recreate what others had already done.

"Well?" she asked, though I was guessing she knew what I'd been thinking. Whether that was through her own magic or common sense I doubted I'd ever know.

"I shouldn't be learning Everard's way," I answered.

"Correct. Everard is a showman, brash and charming, able to convince others of his vision. You are an artificer. Magic for you won't be a system of words and gestures or runes inscribed on an object. Your magic is directly tied to your essence. It will work when it joins with your other skills."

"It sounds like you are telling me to use blacksmithing to do magic," I said.

"All the mages who've wielded power through the ages have had their own specialty that made them unique. Quinn, you design and build devices. Let the magic flow through you and into your work, and you will know success."

"Thank you, Maelyrra."

She acknowledged me with a slight dip of her chin. "If

you would allow me, I'd like to show you one thing before I leave you."

"Of course."

She held out her hand to me and I grasped it gently, afraid my metal hand would damage the delicate woman. A cool sense of peace and harmony flowed into me and lifted my spirits. I hadn't realized how much grief and anger I'd been carrying until it was taken off my shoulders. Without a word or a gesture, we shifted into a dark room somewhere other than Treetop. The room's only feature was a spinning blue globe the size of a cart that cast enough light to push the shadows back, but not dispel them.

"Where are we?" I asked as I stared at the globe, noticing the scudding clouds, the rippling waves of the ocean. Astaria opened out before me, from the northern reaches of Terralon to the high plains of the Candalarian Horde spread out to the south. The Norn Empire stood off to the northeast of Terralon. I circled the globe, but the rest was hazy and nondescript.

"We are on my plane of existence. The source of Astarian's magic bound by the alarium in the ground under your country." Her voice sounded miles away and yet so close that I expected her to be next to me.

"This is our world, but I can't see what else is here."

"There is much you do not know, and I cannot reveal things about the world you have not learned on your own." The globe spun and grew until I stood outside Lapis the night of the bear attack. Everything was frozen in place, but I could walk around the scene. Maelyrra stood next to me as I studied the details I hadn't had time to notice in the middle of the fight.

"Magic takes all forms, Quinn." Her gentle voice was the only sound. "You are on a path to either save us or doom us to the darkness. Fate has chosen you to be her tool in righting what once went wrong."

Me? I didn't want to believe her, but it was Lady Maelyrra. Magic emanated off her like heat from a forge. I felt an urge to protect her at any cost, making it impossible to deny her. I'd come to realize there must be a reason she chose me. I'd have to trust her judgment until it became clear that I could do the job. "What do I need to do?"

"You will know when the time comes, but you cannot do this alone. Pick your allies carefully, for there are forces at work seeking to end the light for good."

"Is the bear attack part of it?" I asked, my voice hesitant. The enormity of it all set my head spinning. "If I find the responsible party, will the threat be over?"

"I think not. This may have ties to the enemy, but may only be coincidental." She stared off into the darkness for a moment before continuing. "The future is unclear, but you are resourceful and strong."

As we stood in the dark outside of Lapis, watching the bear dragging the magus's corpse across the ground, I felt neither strong nor resourceful. Then an idea struck me. I fumbled in my pouch, producing the rune-covered device I'd taken from the bear. I held it out to her. "My Lady, do you know what this is?"

Her eyes widened as her fingers touched the piece. "This is strong magic. Where did you get it?"

"It was in the box controlling the bear. Watcher Wyndham analyzed the liquid I found in the box along with this. It turns out it is a drug that puts the victim into a hypnotic state. Someone was forcing the bear to kill people."

Maelyrra flipped the device, studying the engravings. "It is not of our type of magic," she said after a while. "My guess is a Candalarian Wind Walker enchanted it. The Norns use runes but these are not theirs. It is complex magic meant to be cast from a distance, but I can glean nothing else."

It was more than I'd had before. If the bear controller was in league with the Candalarian Horde, it made sense the attacks happened on the border between Candalar and Astaria. If this was the start of a larger invasion, more attacks would be coming and I'd need to be prepared to face them. I was about to ask Lady Maelyrra to return me to Treetop when something caught my eye.

I strode across the ground to examine the bear more closely. The images felt real enough that I half expected the bear to attack me. It had torn the arm from the magus who had tried to stop it. The arm, wrapped in the metal armature the magi used to emulate magic, dripped blood onto the grass under the bear. Why that body—why that part of the body? What if it was after the technology? Had the same happened at the other two towns or if the attack was meant to lure the magus out to fight the bear?

If they were after the artifacts and not just killing villagers, this changed everything.

13

My mind flooded with all new questions. Who would benefit from stealing the magus' gear? What were they using it for? Why employ an animal instead of ambushing a magus and taking what they wanted? Too many unknowns and no answers.

Maelyrra returned us to Treetop without a word or a gesture. "I know the path may be difficult for you, but you will grow into a tremendous mage."

In the blink of an eye, Maelyrra was gone and I was alone with my thoughts. How does being an artificer lend itself to magic? I built devices, not magic spells.

Everard emerged from the hallway carrying two mugs, Jabber following closely behind him with a tray of food. "Good to see you are back. Jabber and I prepared dinner since you can't work on an empty stomach."

To illustrate the point, my stomach growled at the smell of roasted chicken and potatoes. I pushed the papers to the side, making room for the meal. Everard placed a mug of ale in front of me. I took a quick drink while Jabber set out the food. I noticed the clock on the wall and flinched. "I didn't realize I'd been gone all day."

Everard nodded, setting down his food. "What did you and Maelyrra discuss, if you don't mind me asking?"

I reviewed our conversation, told him of the room with the globe, and how we'd watched the scene of the bear attack. He interjected a couple of questions for clarification as I went. In the end, we came to the same conclusion—the attacks were intended to steal the alarium powered magus armaments.

Jabber interrupted me. "Master Quinn, your food is getting cold and you've not eaten today."

My mother had died when I was a child, but now I had a mechanical mother to watch over me. Obediently I bit into the chicken, juice running down my chin.

Everard groaned. "We should teach you table manners." I started to protest, but he cut me off. "You eat. I'll talk." He took a swig of his ale as Jabber cleared his plate. "I need you to make me an automaton."

"It's not all it's cracked up to be," I said with a snort.

"I heard that." Jabber's voice came from down the hall. "You would be lost without me to take care of Treetop."

Everard chuckled. "He's got you there. Over the years, Maelyrra has shown up to speak to me a handful of times, and only twice have I been invited to the viewing chamber. Both were when Astaria was in the most danger."

"Viewing chamber?"

"The place with the globe in it. It is a powerful artifact that brings you to what you need to see most. This situation must be important for her to take you this early in your training."

"I still don't know how to use my magic any better than I did, and now you are telling me the situation is worse than we'd guessed. None of this is making me feel any better."

"Tell me again what Maelyrra said about learning magic," Everard said.

"She said I need to approach it as if it was an artificer's problem."

"How would you solve any other problems?"

I scratched my chin as I thought. "I'd examine the problem, decide what tool I needed to fix the issue."

"Exactly," Everard said, reaching across to fill my mug. "Let's start with something easier than the bear and all that. Design something to lift a box."

"But I need to—"

"No, just a device to lift something. Build a machine and let me know when it's ready. No arguments, just do it."

I started to disagree that I didn't have time to waste, but until the hidden enemy made his next move, I had nothing but time. As my old Master Blacksmith used to say, you had to build the fire before you could bend metal, and he was right. "I'll get on it."

"Good." Everard left the room.

I retrieved my sketch pad and began to draw new plans for a lifting device. Jabber collected my dishes, placed an alarium lamp on the table, and retired to the other side of the room in case I needed anything.

Hours passed as I designed a piece to attach to my left arm gauntlet. It was a flattened cylinder with a dial so I could adjust how high I wanted to raise the object. I went into the workshop and lit the forge fire. I started with rough shaping the pieces of the lifter. Energy flowed through and around me as I worked, setting the hairs on my arm on edge. I'd never experienced anything like that before. My focus was razor-sharp, noticing small imperfections in the metal.

Jabber silently operated the bellows as I cast the base from bronze. Once the clay mold was filled, I used silver stock to craft the dial. I wasn't sure how the magic I could now feel would be incorporated, but I was too focused for such concerns to affect me. Everard said to build a device and I was making it, even though I wondered if it would work.

Swirls of energy spun around me while I hammered out the forms even as an icy sensation covered my body. Invisible strands bound me to each piece I created. Somehow it was as if they were alive in my mind. Was this how Everard felt when he did his magic? As I worked, the completed form hung in my mind like a kite on the wind. I knew it would work.

I set the silver disc aside and broke open the clay mold to examine the casted piece. It needed to be smoothed out for easy turning, but it was not cracked or warped. I drafted a small hole through the bottom for the pin that would bring the two pieces together. Once the screw was done, I heated the silver and set the thread pattern so when it cooled the two pieces would connect.

"Master Quinn, you should go to bed," Jabber said as I dozed in the armchair outside the workshop waiting for the pieces to be ready.

I stretched and stifled a yawn. "I'm going to put the pieces together and then I'll go to bed." Sleep would have to wait. I wanted to see if the device I made did anything at all.

My energy waned with each passing moment. I felt drained to the point of collapse, but I forced myself to keep going. The burden of failure and worry hung over me like a storm cloud. The metal looked cold, but metal was unforgiving and a piece hot enough to burn you looked the same as a cold piece. Once I ensured they were room temperature, I picked them up.

I staggered to the finishing bench with a strong alarium lamp and a magnifying glass for delicate crafting. The creation of weapons, lamps, and other devices required finesse to ensure everything interfaced smoothly. I spent longer than I should have cleaning up the screw threads, but my eyes could barely focus through the bleariness. It did make threading the screw into the housing a lot more difficult.

"Master Quinn," Jabber said. "Might you be better off waiting to finish until you've slept?"

"I would, Jabber, but it's done." At last, the thread caught in the hole dial. I tightened the screw and turned the dial. Nothing happened. I concentrated and pointed the device at the screwdriver on the table. "Lift," I said as I rotated the dial. Still nothing.

Lack of sleep, frustration, and failure were like a strong drink when you've already had too much. I threw the piece onto the floor.

"I'm going to bed." I stumbled out of the workshop, ignoring Jabber, who continued to call my name as I skulked down the hall. *Once a failure, always a failure.*

I reached my room, opened the door, and slammed it behind me. Maelyrra and Everard had told me to use my artificing to access my magic, and I'd come up short. You didn't find the defects in your metal until you heated it. Well, the heat of the forge had brought my flaws to the surface and I'd cracked.

Now, I dreaded the hammer strike that would shatter me.

14

BOOM! BOOM! BOOM!

I pulled the heavy blanket over my head to blot out the noise of Everard knocking, not that it was doing much good. Thoughts of my failed device pushed at me, but I shoved them away and tried to go back to sleep.

BOOM! BOOM! BOOM!

I tossed the blankets off and stormed to the door, throwing it open so that it crashed into the wall. "What?" I yelled at the startled Arch Magus, failure and lack of sleep replacing my healthy fear of the man.

"Good morning, Quinn," he said, a quirked eyebrow the only sign he found my behavior less than acceptable. "I'd like for you to explain something to me. If you don't mind, follow me."

I held my head in both hands, trying to squeeze the headache out. What could be so important that he couldn't leave me to sleep? "Let me put on some clothes first."

He glanced down and I followed his gaze. I still wore the forge-scented, wrinkled, sweaty clothes from yesterday. I groaned as I added washing my bedding to my list of chores. "Fine. Let's go."

What was this about? Had he found the useless device in pieces on the floor? The last thing I needed this morning was a lecture on how to relax my center so I could do better magic. "Everard, I'm not a mage, I'm a blacksmith. Lady Maelyrra was wrong about me."

The abandoned project lay on the workshop table. A mug of tea sat in front of one of the stools. He gestured for me to take the seat with the tea.

"This one didn't work?" Everard said.

I shrugged wearily, unwilling to look him in the face. Maelyrra had even visited our realm to help me and I'd still failed. I wanted to scream or hit something or maybe just leave. A war raged in my head of all the feelings I couldn't express.

"It was your first attempt," Everard said as he spun the dial. "My first spell took me months of practice before I could do anything of consequence. Light a candle, lift a napkin, were easy."

I really wasn't in the mood for the 'better luck next time' speech. Everard's failures were far behind him. I sipped the tea and stayed silent.

"Do you know why Maelyrra gave you magic?"

"Because I saved you." I hated the sulky tone in my voice, but I couldn't push past the sense of failure.

"No," he said, a sad smile playing across his face. "I'm dying. The magic requires a price and soon it will end me. I've held it off until a replacement could be found, but my time is almost done here. You don't need to be Arch Magus, but you will need to protect Astaria."

My mouth dropped open like a starving man staring at a haunch of lamb. First Roland and now Everard. Was everyone who came into contact with me jinxed? "Can't Lady Maelyrra fix it?"

He snorted a laugh. "There is nothing to fix. My body is worn out and rotting on the inside. In a couple of months, I'll be dead."

Dark circles ringed Everard's normally youthful eyes. I hadn't noticed the ashen skin and the stoop of his shoulders like he carried a great burden on his back. The realization hit me with the force of a forge hammer in the head. I was a blacksmith, not a magus. How in the world could I learn to protect the whole country, when I'd barely learned the basics of being a Watcher? "There has to be a mistake…"

"You know in your heart there isn't," Everard said, affixing me with a penetrating gaze. "Lady Maelyrra could have chosen anyone, but it was you she chose to follow me as the protector of Astaria. I have spent hundreds of years protecting the land I love, and now you will succeed me. You have the potential to be very powerful."

Powerful? Me? I wasn't suited for this kind of power, but would I want it granted to one of the petty magi that squabbled over supposed slights and pouted when they didn't get their way? No. My whole life, I'd been taught that hard work and keeping your word was more important than my pride. "If I don't take the Arch Magus title, who will?"

"Usorin will ascend—"

"What?" I shouted, rising as rapidly as my anger. "The maniac who cut my arm off is going to be Arch Magus? He doesn't even have any magic."

Everard held up his hands and I returned to my seat, glaring at the older man. He cleared his throat. "Arch Magus is a governing term, not a rank granted though ability. Most of Astaria's greatest mages were unknown to the people. Usorin is much changed since he attacked you. He's mellowed and takes his place far more seriously now. You have the option of stepping up to be the next Arch Magus if you so choose. Once you display your power, no one will question you. Think about it, though. Do you want to give up this life to be tied to governing Astaria?"

I'd thought of what it had to be like to spend all day managing the thirteen regions and foreign disputes. Political intrigue, boot lickers, and all the rest that Everard put up with. Not for me. "I'm not cut out to lead. Usorin will have to be the one who takes over."

Everard shrugged. "He's one of the few that know the true secret of alarium. He won't trouble you regardless of your decision."

"Without magic, there is no decision," I insisted, trying not to let the hurt and anger into my voice. I failed.

"Do this for me. Try again. Pick something to work on. Think about what you want to happen and how it should feel when it succeeds. Traces of magic fluxed through the pieces of the device. You just need to find what inside you will fuse them together to achieve your goal."

He was right. I could sit here feeling sorry for myself or I could get back to it. "What happens if I can't get it to work?"

"Nothing," Everard said after a moment. "My guess is Lady Maelyrra makes few mistakes, but she will pick a new champion if you are unable to take over."

The thought of losing my magic, even though it eluded me, was appealing and terrifying at the same time. As much as the magic frustrated me, I wanted to protect the people of Astaria. Victoria said we each have skills to contribute. I'd continue building weapons to protect the people, but not to the extent that Everard had. I couldn't build a weapon big enough to take out an entire Norn fleet or shatter an invading Candelaria army. To do that I needed my magic. "I've got to get the levitator to work."

"You'll be a great mage. Trust in yourself. I certainly

believe in you. Maelyrra wouldn't have chosen you if you weren't worthy."

"Will you be here later?"

"No," Everard said slowly. "I'm afraid this will probably be the last time I speak with you. Even now I can feel my body deteriorating. I used most of my magic to come here and have just enough to return home."

I nodded, feeling my heart break. The older man hugged me tightly in yet another goodbye. Yet another death. He whispered something in my ear and the world went dark. When I woke up in bed later, he was gone.

"Thank you, Everard."

15

With renewed determination, I returned to the levitator. The original model went into my slag pile so I could melt it down later. I selected a couple of stock pieces, examining each piece carefully. Everard had spoken about "feeling" the magic and seeing the transformation I wanted. Nothing.

I selected a couple more pieces and tried the same thing. Still nothing.

"Excuse me," Jabber said from the doorway.

I'd been so deep in concentration, I hadn't heard him approach. With a small jolt of shock, I dropped the pieces on the floor. I bent down to retrieve the metal. "What is it?"

"I was wondering if you'd be breaking for lunch?"

"No," I said. My left hand grasped the fallen stock and I gasped. A shock ran up my arm. I moved the piece to my right hand and the sensation ended. I'd been using my artificial arm to touch the metal I'd worked with.

I switched the metal back to my left hand and the jolt of energy almost caused me to drop it again. I straightened, examining the metal. Pulses of magic ran up and down my arm. Without warning my skin began to ripple under an unseen force. Blue energy seeped out of the skin from my hand to my elbow. A torrent of force flowed into the metal with me being pulled along like a rider with a foot stuck in the stirrup of a galloping horse. I willed my grip to loosen, but my fingers were welded to the metal. The glow from my arm intensified until I could no longer look at it. With a deafening crack, the metal burst into shards falling to the floor.

"Are you ill?" Jabber asked. If his eyes could have widened I'm sure they would have.

"I'm fine." A wave of fatigue struck me like a sledge-hammer driving spikes sending me to my knees. Jabber caught me before I fell completely. He carefully escorted me to my room. I was asleep before my head hit the pillow.

A few hours later, I pulled myself out of bed and stumbled to the kitchen. I grabbed an apple and some cheese which was gone before I realized I'd eaten it. After a second apple, I felt more like myself. Time to see what I'd created earlier.

The door to the workshop stood open. I entered and saw the remains of the metal stock I'd touched earlier. It pulsed a pale blue light around it. Well, at least I hadn't dreamed it. My left arm looked normal.

"No time like the present," I said into the quiet of the shop. I selected a new piece of metal with my forging arm, sensing the design I was planning wanting to emerge from the bar. I set the piece on the anvil and touched it with one finger. A tiny trickle of energy leapt out and encompassed the stock. I pulled my hand away not wanting a repeat of my earlier experience. The glow faded after a few moments. I tried again, touching the piece longer to allow more magic to pour into the inert metal. After a couple of hours of trial and error, the metal glowed like it had been pulled from the forge.

I grabbed my tongs and the rounding hammer and set to work. The metal responded like it had been properly heated, but wasn't hot to the touch.

I set to making a new levator, sensing the difference in the metal, the forms buried inside beckoning to be released. For the next day, I labored over the device, taking a short break to eat and sleep. Finally, I held the new device in my hand. "Jabber, come here, please."

Jabber appeared in the doorway after a minute. "Yes, Master Quinn."

I pointed the levitator at Jabber and turned the dial. He rose a few inches off the floor. I snapped off the dial, whooping in joy. Finally, I knew it was working.

I'd done it. I did have the magic Lady Maelyrra had granted me. I was worthy.

"Master Quinn, that was unexpected," Jabber said, his tone tinged with disapproval.

I grabbed him by the arms. "Jabber, it worked! It worked!" I danced around the shop, using the levitator to pick up and drop things back on the bench. Everard would be so proud if he were here.

I spent the next week building on a device to neutralize the hypnosis machine. Everard trusted me to stop these people, and I refused to let them win. If it took every drop of blood in my body, I'd complete the last mission he'd given me.

After a lot of bad designs, I settled on a pistol to deliver the magic. This way I could pinpoint the animal and disrupt the hypnosis. I crafted a pistol body, envisioning the spell fired like a bullet and calibrated the trigger. I certainly didn't want an area effect for the magic, since I had no way of determining what would happen. The directional vector of the pistol design should limit the effective field. The main problem was that I couldn't test it. The control device from the bear lay in pieces since I'd removed most of the parts to study it. I wouldn't know if it worked until I faced down the next monstrosity.

Over the next week, I created a freeze bomb. It took a while to build the spherical casing so when I pressed the button and threw it, it would freeze everything in place after two seconds. The Norns used firebombs to soften up defenses, but my bomb should halt an opponent in their tracks for at least thirty seconds. Literally. It would have been handy against the bear.

After three tries I was setting the firing pin in my new bomb design when Jabber entered. He held the neutralizing pistol I'd left on the table. "Master Quinn, I'm looking at the plans for your newest project and I have a few suggestions for improvements."

The liquid bronze in the crucible bubbled and steamed. I poured it carefully into the spherical mold, each half ready to lock together around the activation button. Without taking my eyes off the casting I said, "Those are old. The final plans are on the workbench."

He laid the old plans down and retrieved the new ones, studying them carefully. "This won't work."

I groaned. Jabber took full advantage of his freedom to discuss things ad nauseum. I finished the pour and straightened. "Why is that, Jabber?"

He pointed at the pistol device I'd created earlier. "The trigger mechanism is not correct. See the second pin here? It should be further back to balance the force of the trigger pull. This could break if any torque is applied during the firing of the weapon."

I frowned. "The trigger isn't connected to any other

mechanical parts, so the resistance is low enough to avoid torque. With black powder pistols, the trigger has to be secured, but this is for magic."

"The application doesn't change the fact that the trigger is not properly reinforced to allow for the user to hastily fire the weapon as one would in a combat situation. Master Roland espoused the adage 'Better to over plan than under-deliver.' And in this case, moving the pin would alleviate the stress point and ensure a smooth mechanical function."

He had a point. The fix wouldn't take long, and the last thing I needed was a mechanical failure in the field on top of trying to learn magic. "You're right."

"Besides, given the mechanical hand…" Jabber fell silent. "Did you say I'm right?"

"Yes," I said, fighting to keep the grin off my face. For all Jabber did to maintain Treetop and me, he was childlike in his perception of the world and the strange people in it. "You brought up some good ideas. I'll make the change now."

"Thank you, Master Quinn," he said, sitting on the stool by the workbench.

I retrieved the pistol from the holster I'd found in the weapons locker. Removing the pin involved some swearing and a couple of failed attempts, but I eventually tapped it out. I verified it was still structurally sound, re-drilled the hole through the trigger assembly, and completed the revision. Jabber didn't speak through the whole process, just watched my every move.

"Jabber, feel free to make any suggestions you find necessary. I might not agree with them, but I'd rather discuss it than miss something. A man can't see his own blind spots."

Jabber nodded, rose, and exited the workshop. As he went, I swear he stood a bit straighter. I went back to work.

The sun had set by the time I'd popped the sphere out of the mold so I could file down the rough edges and assemble it. Jabber entered, though this time he didn't carry any of my plans. "Master Quinn, Watcher Cian has requested you meet him in Bradenbridge in two days. There has been another attack on Oriatia, near the Aldon border."

How fast could I finish up here? The freezing orb, as I'd come to think of it, needed a few more hours before it would be ready. To reach Bradenbridge in two days would require leaving early in the morning, but I could forego some sleep in order to complete the orb. Depending on what we were facing, it could come in handy. "1 hour to go before I'm done here. Can you pack my rucksack and layout my combat arm and the new gauntlet?"

"Absolutely, Master Quinn," Jabber said softly. "I will attend to Treetop in your absence. I hope it won't be a long one."

"Me, too," I told him and realized I meant it. Treetop had become home and Jabber was part of that. Did he get lonely here by himself? Surely not. Automatons didn't have feelings, at least I didn't think so, but the image of Jabber walking out, head held high after I'd complimented his suggestions, made me question that.

"Very well," he said crisply, the old Jabber reasserting himself. "I'll have your things ready for your morning departure." After he left, I affixed the button to the sphere casing. I'd built the button to trigger the magic, hoping it would work like the levitation wheel I'd added to my gauntlet.

I wasn't sure if any of my gadgets would affect a rampaging, hypnotized bear or anything else the madman behind this threw at me. If worse came to worse, my mechanical arm and gauntlet and the artificer tricks I'd built into them would come in handy.

I always had my wits if things really went bad. I hoped it never got there.

Because then I was really in trouble.

Three days later, Cian and I rode horses from Herot's Pass into Oriatia and the small town of Bexley's Crossing. From what Cian had said, the town was a bridge over the Itugar River and not much else. The Oriatian magus, Eva Pelham, had reported an attack against her men on the road outside of the village. Pelham had been scheduled to return by carriage from her mountain home to her estates but had taken an airship when her father fell ill.

"We've got a long journey, and we've got time to kill," Cian said as the sun passed noon time and started her journey toward the mountains. "I know you worked with Roland. How did he find you?"

I told him the story of Usorin cutting off my arm and Roland finding me barely alive. I regaled him with the boring details of building my new arm, the more interesting parts of fighting the Norns, and the heartbreaking events around the murder of Master Ruari and the rest of the blacksmiths. I left out Walden Ovro's attempted assassination of Everard as we'd agreed to not discuss Ovro trying to steal Everard's magic and Lady Maelyrra bestowing magic of my own. Though the Watchers "knew" I had magic, they didn't know how or why the magic worked.

"Interesting." We rode for a few minutes in silence. The slope of a large hill slowed our progress but pushing the horses into a trot up an incline would wear them out. "When did you get magic? You didn't mention it earlier in your story."

I'd hoped he'd ignored the omission. Cian was a fellow Watcher, but I didn't want the knowledge about how I got my magic public. "Everard thinks I always had it, but the stress of stopping the fight and the deaths of the people I loved brought it out. Whatever happened, I'm not very good at it." I left out the 'I can build magic items' information.

Cian nodded. "Makes sense. The Wind Walker of the White Ghosts think all souls are magic and we are projections of our true beings. Those who connect to their true selves can bring the magic here. Maybe they are right."

"White Ghosts?"

Cian snorted. "They barely have any skin coloring."

"Do you know a lot about the Candalarians?"

"Enough," Cian said with a sigh. "Guess you don't know 'bout me." He glanced at me, and when I agreed he kept going. "Old Brull was the Watcher in Ramcoll when I was a boy. When I was young, the Candalarians bought, or stole, me from my parents and made me a slave. That's how I learned their language. I was being auctioned off near the border to Astarian farmers—"

"Wait," I interrupted. "Slaves are illegal in Astaria. The Norns and Candalarians allow it, but anyone in our country would be freed."

"Quinn, you haven't been a Watcher long, but out on the plains of Aldon and Ramcoll, there's no law other than the magus and they are more interested in taxes on grain and corn sales to look too closely at who does the farming." Cian tried to smile, but it wavered.

"The farmers in Bradenbridge don't use slaves," I countered. I'd known many of the local farmers as an apprentice blacksmith before I'd become a watcher.

"Maybe not. But a few hours' ride south of Iron Harbor you'll find Thaclet. It's the largest slave market on the continent. Some of the slaves the Norns sell end up in Terralon."

I'd spent my whole life in Bradenbridge and the subject never came up. Granted, the farm holdings were hours away from the city, but the farmers ventured to town frequently to sell their goods and buy supplies. Ruari had repaired and maintained farm implements all winter long to ready them for the spring. "I've never seen any slaves or heard rumor of them."

Cian held up his hands. "I haven't been to your neck of the woods, so I don't know for a fact. Just tellin' you what I heard."

As unpalatable as it was, I couldn't see any reason for Cian to lie about it. "Why don't the Watchers free the slaves?"

"Brull drove it into my head that we weren't here to fight every evil in the world, but to keep Astaria safe. I concentrate on the mission at hand regardless of my feelings."

"And Brull?"

"He died in a fight with a White Ghost Wind Walker. Everard promoted me to Ramcoll's Watcher. I've been here ever since."

Like me, someone else's death had been involved in his promotion. How had Victoria Wyndham been recruited into the Watchers? I'd have to ask her when I saw her next. The idea of him being a slave rattled me like a loose screw in a perambulator. I'd seen excesses and cruelty from the magus of Bradenbridge, but we were all free. If Ruari hadn't taken me in and taught me a craft, I could have ended up on a farm, worked to the bone, though at least I wouldn't have been a slave.

Cian cleared his throat. "Anyhow, Brull taught me to read and how to hunt. Being able to track across the grasslands is a skill few possess, so I can use it in service to protect people. I can track the White Ghosts when they enter into our territory. When they cross into Astaria I can hunt them down."

"Does that happen often?

"In Ramcoll it does. Mostly raids on livestock. Occasionally they try to kidnap people for ransom or to be sold off. Most of the farmers have walled compounds to keep themselves safe."

What a difference from Bradenbridge, though the port city Cheim sported walls to keep the Norn raiding ships from entering the harbor. Astaria was a country with enemies, and our mission as Watchers was to protect the citizens and keep the rulers of the regions in line. "What do you do when that happens?"

Cian's grin reminded me of a wolf. "I rescue the Astarians and kill as many of the bastards I can in the process."

"What does Everard say about all this?"

Cian's eyes swept the area around us while he slowed his horse to get him around a large hole in the path. "I don't know and don't care. The White Ghosts are animals who kill and maim without provocation, and it's our job to keep rabid animals away from Astaria."

I was about to answer when the thunder of hoofbeats rolled over the hill ahead of us.

And that was when the Candalarians showed up.

Four warriors on large black horses crested the hill, facing us. Cian and I readied ourselves for a fight, angling our horses until we were side by side. The animals shied and pranced from the sudden intrusion. The Candalarians were known to be fierce warriors who rode their horses like they were born in the saddle. An array of lances, bows, and a couple of swords stuck out in all directions? The warriors were clad in leathers, but the horses were decorated with bright colors and baubles. I stopped examining them when I realized one of them had a string of fingers around his horse's neck. I readied my arm while the riders moved to flank us.

"This isn't good," Cian muttered.

I grunted in response. Which one was the leader? If they attacked and I killed their leader, the rest might think better of harassing us, though the odds of that were about the same as steam billowing out of my nose.

And that was a device I hadn't invented yet.

The largest of the warriors with broad shoulders, long

black hair, and a beard down to his waist cautiously approached us. His white skin shimmered in the sunlight. I now understood where the term 'White Ghost' came from. It was like the inside of an oyster shell.

He held up the spear and the rest of the riders spread themselves equally behind him to ensure they had room to maneuver. He studied us for a long moment before he spoke. "I Dakao. We speak of you. Looking for our Huallia."

"Huallia?" I asked Cian. The leader sat tall in the saddle, but he must have been shorter than me. Height wasn't necessary for riding horses, and the smooth way he guided his with his knees proved that fact.

"It means Wind Walker," Cian whispered before responding to their leader. "Ja latta non Huallia. Ju gryra jey truio."

"What did you say?

"I told him we didn't see their Wind Walker and to leave our lands."

Dakao laughed as did his men. "You not speak as warrior." He addressed me, dismissing Cian. "We seek Huallia. Gema-ki." He indicated the warrior to his left. She nodded her head in my direction, but I kept my eyes fastened on Dakao. "The Wind Walkers take us to place and find metal arm man." It sounded like he said kin in his broken Astarian, but I knew he meant me.

As hard as I tried, I couldn't stop Cian's hard words from echoing in my mind. These were the people who sold him as a slave and still did so today. Was he wrong to want to kill them on sight? If I ever found them selling a human I know I would burn them to the ground. Under the circumstances, I needed to follow where this was leading.

Cian bristled. "I told you to leave our lands. You have no right to be here."

"We not speak to slave, we search for our Huallia," Dakao said in a casual tone.

His cheeks flamed red at the insult. "We are Ostarian guards and I demand you leave."

This wasn't going well. If I didn't step in, Cian would rise to the provocation and blood would be shed. I pulled back my sleeve to expose the metal of my arm. "I am Quinn, but I have no information on your missing Wind Walker."

Gemaki answered instead of the leader. "You will lead and we will find Huallia."

I inspected each member of the group. Dark circles, like iron rings, hung under their eyes, blotching their pale skin. Their leathers were matted with dirt and sweat, telling me they'd been searching for a while. Cian muttered to himself as I examined the situation and came to a decision. "It is getting dark. Let us camp for the night and discuss what to do."

Cian whispered. "I'm not spending the night with these savages."

Dakao ignored Cian and swung off his horse. He approached me, his arm extended. I looked at him, wondering what I should do.

"I offer peace on my ancestors, Quinn of Astaria," Dakao said simply, his arm still reaching for mine.

Cian sighed. "Grip his arm at the elbow and repeat the words."

I clambered down from my saddle, a landslide to the flowing water of Dakao's dismount. I took his arm and repeated the words as his calloused hand gripped my elbow. The leader then pulled me close and kissed me full on the mouth.

"What?" I stammered, caught completely off-guard.

Cian laughed as Dakao said, "We have shared breath. We are as family until the next moon rises."

I cast a sour look at Cian, who tried to smother his grin. "You knew about that, didn't you?"

The older man kept grinning. "I told you they were savages. I'll not break bread with these murderers."

I pushed the urge to test my freeze bomb on Cian out of my mind. I pushed down the uneasy feeling that had settled over me. "They don't appear to be hostile, just looking for their Wind Walker."

"Quinn, you're a fool. They would as soon murder you as spit on you. We need to leave now." Cian's voice was hot with anger.

"You need to go back to Herot's Pass and send a report to Everard." I couldn't have Cian causing bloodshed because of his personal grudge, even though he had every right to hate these people. Was I being a fool for not just killing them instead of working with them?

"What?" Cian said, almost at a shout, drawing the looks of the Candalarians. "You can't be serious."

"I am. They will follow us if I leave with you, but we need Everard to know so he can send more Watchers."

Cian scowled. "Quinn, this isn't smart."

"It's the only way this works. I'll help them search while you get help." I sounded crazy even to myself, but there was no way they had heard of me through non-magical means. There was something here and I needed to stop the attacks. That had to take priority even over my own safety.

After a long moment, Cian agreed. "I'll ride to Herot's Pass and come back with more men to even the odds."

"It's settled. You head out and I'll wait for you."

Cian wheeled his horse around and rode off the way we had come. Once he was gone, I approached Candalarians. "We should find shelter for the night."

I followed the riders into a small copse of trees at the base of the hill where we found a clearing to make camp in.

Dakao's people started a fire and placed reed mats around the far side of it. I set out my tarp and blankets, glad to be in the temperate southern portion of Astaria. As fall crept closer to winter, sleeping outside became less and less pleasant.

I pulled a pan to cook the bacon and beans I'd packed. Across the fire, I saw each of the warriors gnawing on pieces of meat with no cooking utensils in sight. Cian had mentioned they don't cook their food. With a huff, I stored the bacon and beans, pulled out some jerky, and joined Dakao's people with my meal.

As I approached, Gemaki waved to the patch of ground next to her. I nodded my thanks and sat near enough to her to talk, but not so close as be within reach. She smiled as she looked at the space between us. After a moment she held out a piece of the meat she was eating.

"No, thank you," I said as I shook my head so she'd understand. The thought of eating raw meat did nothing for my appetite. She pushed it toward me more emphatically. With the realization that refusal could be seen as an insult, I smiled and took the proffered meat. She waited until I tore a piece off with my teeth.

I chewed the meat, which tasted peppery and carried a bit of heat. Rather than being tough, it fell apart easily as I ate it. "This is good," I told her between mouthfuls of the spicy meat.

"Why did Golacka leave?"

My brows knit together as I tried to puzzle out the meaning of the word. Gemaki gave me the answer.

"Low-born. He speaks the tongue of the fields."

"He went to report to our master." She meant slave, but I didn't correct her. We ate in silence as the sun slowly dissolved behind the mountains. I handed her my water skin which she took a long pull from, as did I. The heat on my tongue intensified as I ate the food.

"The charga cooks the meat while we ride and does not destroy the animal's spirit as fire does. Those who are spirit-blind do not see the dishonor in putting meat on the flame. We weep for those such as you."

That might have been the nicest insult I'd ever received. I had nearly finished our shared meal when it dawned on me I had an expert sitting next to me. The device I'd found was supposedly Candalarian magic. It was a risk to be sure, but what if the risk paid off? I wiped my hands on my pants and retrieved the leather pouch from my belt.

Gemaki's eyes followed my every move as I extracted the device and held it in my palm. "Do you know what this is?"

Her eyes grew as large as quenching barrels as she scrambled away from me. Gemaki screamed something in her language and the other Candalarians pulled weapons and jumped between us. I stood, sliding the box into my pocket.

Dakao's face darkened in the flickering light of the fire as he stared at me, spear in hand. I readied for a fight, but I needed answers, not bloodshed. I held up my hands in front of me. This was getting out of control quickly.

"I'm sorry. I found this on a bear that had been turned into a killing machine. I need to know what it is before it happens again."

A series of conversations flowed between the four Candalarians. Gemaki's voice still held a tremble of fear as she answered Dakao's questions.

I eased back away from the group and out of stabbing distance of Dakao's wicked-looking spear.

After a few minutes, Dakao returned without his spear. "We talk in morning. Evil best not talked in dark." He went back to his people who sat huddled together, whispering frantically.

I sat watching the Candalarians and the dark. What in the hell was this device, that it terrified hardened warriors such as these?

I wondered which I should be more scared of, the Candarlians or the device that scared them.

The sun rose over our strange camp. Dakao's band ate breakfast and stored their belongings. Gemaki watched me from beyond her people as I packed my gear and gnawed on hardtack. If the Candalarians didn't open up discussions of what had happened last night soon, I would have to do it myself.

Dakao strolled across the intervening space, his gait swaying from spending so much time in the saddle. He stopped at a respectful distance.

I felt my shoulders tighten with anxiety.

"Quinn, I explain. The piece is evil. Soul Stealers control people with such things, make do horrible things. Where get it?"

I told him the story of the bear. "I am sorry to have startled Gemaki. I had no idea what it was to you."

"It is you not understanding. I speak with my people." He returned to the Candalarians. He wore a metal breastplate over his coat this morning. In fact, they all did. Seeing the evil magic had certainly shaken them to the core. Their hands lingered on their weapons now, where last night they had relaxed.

As Dakao spoke, Gemaki's eyes flicked back and forth from him to me. She scowled and fired off a string of words that, from the tone of them, should have burnt Dakao to the ground. He weathered the storm with a calm I found amazing. The other two warriors, Mojuro and Akaru, stood to the side. Mojuro had strung his bow, Akaru spun throwing knives around his fingers as he listened.

I brushed down my horse, checked his shoes, pulling out pebbles with the tip of my metal finger. After a once over, I gave him a small apple from my sack. He crunched happily as I stroked his mane.

My morning routine was cut off as Dakao and Gemaki returned. She appraised me. "Quinn, I now know you were stupid as to what the nathal was. It is very evil. If you will give to me, I can follow the evil to the source."

Finally, a break. I'd found someone who could help locate the culprit behind the bear attack. If we removed the people behind the attacks and the drug, we'd never have to face this threat again. The question was could I convince her to lead me to the evil and defeat it?.

"We both want the same thing," I said, keeping my tone as neutral as possible. "I know we are traditionally enemies, but if we work together, we can end this evil once and for all."

The Candalarians agreed.

"May I have the nathal?" Gemaki asked, her hand open before her.

I retrieved the device and gave it to her. Gemaki took a deep breath as if to steady herself before she closed her fingers around it.

"I'm on my way to examine the scene of another attack about a day's ride from here. We think it is connected to the bear attack, but don't know for sure. I'd appreciate your assistance."

"We will follow until we find our Huallia. The spirits have told us so." Dakao said, turning on his heel and returning to his horse.

Gemaki went to do the same but stopped. "Quinn, this is very dangerous. Know this." She headed back, gracefully mounting and bringing her horse around.

I swung up into the saddle and started for Bexley's Crossing. They kept a bit of distance between us as we rode. I turned the problem over and over in my mind, trying to find a link between all the facts I had. None of it made sense.

We ate while we watered the horses. Every hour we dismounted and walked for a bit to conserve their strength. I appreciated the chance to stretch my legs. Gemaki watched me on several occasions, but she turned away if I approached, and Dakao didn't seem to welcome my company so I kept to myself.

We reached a small forest, which according to the map contained the site of the attack. I reigned in my horse to speak with Dakao. "We received a report of a group of guards being ambushed in the woods. I want to examine over the area to see if it is linked to the bear attacks."

Dakao looked up to check the position of the sun. "Can we reach before dark?"

"I think so. I don't know exactly where it happened, but it should be under an hour's ride." I waited for his agreement before starting off again. Something felt wrong, but I couldn't put my finger on just what it was. A case of the jitters, I hoped.

We had been taking the road through the trees for almost an hour when I saw the first body. I dismounted, tying off my horse on a branch. The horse's eyes rolled back as he whinnied. Something besides just the body was spooking him, and that wasn't good. Dakao and his warriors joined me, weapons out and readied. Their horses stood stock still, but their eyes flicked around nervously.

The scene reminded me of the last attack on Murkwood. A carriage with the Pelham crest emblazoned on the doors. Two horses were still attached to the stuck carriage. They snorted and stamped their fear and tried to pull free to no avail. Three men's lifeless bodies littered the ground. Stains where the blood had soaked into the ground surround each person.

The closest body I turned onto his back. The bearded man's throat had been ripped out. I stepped over the corpse and approached the empty carriage the guards had been escorting. Tracks interlaced all over the place, and I moved cautiously as I approached. No sign of the horses, but a man in an Ostarian guard uniform lay on the ground, mauled beyond recognition.

As I examined each person, it was evident that something closely resembling the bear attack had occurred. All had their throats torn out and bite marks riddled their bodies. All these people were killed for no reason.

Dakao joined me. "We need to go. Those wolves markings," he said softly. His spear was held loosely in his right hand, though I was sure he was ready and willing to use it at a moment's notice. His eyes peered into the darkening woods. Animals rustled in the underbrush.

"We'll never reach Bexley's Crossing before nightfall." I removed my coat to prepare my arm and gauntlet for a fight. "We should find a defensible position, secure the horses, and get a fire going."

"Agreed." We walked back to the horses, eyes everywhere as the sounds in the underbrush increased. Within minutes Dakao's people had a small fire burning in the center of the clearing. Mojuro stacked dry tree branches nearby while

Gemaki, stick in hand, circled around the group drawing inscriptions in the dirt.

"Do not step on the wards," she warned, her voice echoing through the near silence of the clearing. A snapping noise from the woods, louder than the pops of the fire caught my attention, but I saw nothing

Gemaki waved everyone inside the circle she'd created and finished the wards. "Stay inside the circle. Your weapons may cross but not your body."

The runes were similar to the ones on the control device I'd taken from the bear. A ripple of power tingled my senses, but it was much different than the feel of my magic. Ghostly apparitions flickered at the corner of my eye but fled when I tried to look at them directly.

The first howl in the distance stopped any thoughts of magical theory. Each of us faced away from the fire, preparing our weapons. Dakao added wood to the fire, increasing the range we could see. I longed to put on my Watcher's mask so I could see better, but I didn't want to give away my identity. The Candalarians were still enemies even if our goals coincided for now.

The sun had gone behind the mountains, plunging the clearing into complete darkness. I wished we were in open land where the moon could illuminate the area, but the canopy filtered the light there was. Red sparks flicked into and out of view as the wolves howled outside the range of our light.

Dakao said, "Those mountain wolves."

Mojuro scoffed. "They are strong but die like anything else.

"The bear we fought took down two magus before we took care of it. We'll be lucky to survive the night if there are a lot of them."

"I can hear they are just wolves." Mojuro sounded less confident than before.

A louder growl came from in front of me as the red, glowing mechanical eyes pushed through the scrub and into the clearing. The wolf was the size of a pony. It loped toward us, unnatural armor reflecting the light. When he reached the circle Gemaki had etched in the ground, it yelped and backed away.

Would it be enough to keep the wolves at bay? And would this be a good time to test my magical devices?

An unbelievably large, armored wolf emerged from the trees and howled, summoning the rest of the pack. They slid like ghosts from the trees, hard to distinguish in the dim light of the fire. The animal growled in greeting. The horses whinnied and thrashed as the scent of the wolves reached them.

"Will the circle hold?" I asked Gemaki, The wolves darted toward us in waves before retreating from the spell.

"I know not," she answered. "I've never warded for beasts such as these."

As if to answer her question, a smaller wolf charged, throwing itself at the barrier. It bounced off the invisible shield. I let out the breath I was holding when the shield flared brightly before subsiding. The alpha stood across from me, its head cocked as if listening to something.

"Get ready," I said when the alpha snapped his teeth. The wolves stormed the circle, striking it with their bodies over and over. I fired lightning, and the arrows and knives from Dakos's people flew through the barrier, hitting the wolves. One wolf reeled to the side and fell, an arrow piercing its right optic.

The alpha charged at Dakao. He rammed his spear through the barrier, attempting to kill the animal. The wolf dodged to the side, latched on to the spear, and dragged the blade down. As the Candalarian leader tried to dislodge his weapon from the wolf, Gemaki screamed, "Do not disturb the wards."

It was too late. The blade scraped on the ground in Gemaki's inscriptions.

The barrier broke apart. The wolves attacked.

I fired my flame weapon at the alpha, forcing him back, but the fire did little more than singe the fur around his armor. He backed off, scared of the flames. I whirled and punched down, striking the wolf who darted in to try to hamstring me. His steel teeth clamped down on my mechanical wrist, but instead of yanking back and possibly losing my arm, I set off the lightning.

The teeth acted as the perfect conductor, frying the wolf before he could do anything. The poor animal slumped to the ground. I hated to kill them since they were being forced to attack us, but I had little choice in the matter.

Around me, the fighting intensified as the wolves darted in and away. They tore at the Candalarians. Mojuro lay on the ground, blood seeping from gashes on his leg. Akaru swung a short sword at two wolves, keeping them at bay, as Gemaki stabbed in from the side. Her sword found a gap between the armor plates and dropped the wolf. Another of the pack dove at the distracted Wind Walker. I fired flames at it, driving the animal back before it could strike.

We'd managed to kill three wolves and lose one of our own and the fight had just started. They seemed to vanish then appeared where I least expected them. The alpha charged at me again. I grabbed the magical pistol from my belt and hoped it would eliminate the control device on the wolf's back. I pulled the trigger and the damn thing snapped under my finger.

When he struck me in the chest, the wolf's momentum carried me backward. He'd have torn out my throat if I hadn't wedged my metal arm between his jaws. I stumbled over the edge of the fire, the wolf on top. Thrusting with all my strength, I propelled the solid creature off of me, leaving a mixture of blood and saliva spattered across me. The animal crashed into the brush as I pulled myself to my feet.

Gemaki swung her sword at another attacker but didn't realize her mistake until too late. As she swung at the first animal, a second sped in and grabbed her leg. She shrieked. The sword tumbled out of her hand, leaving her open for the killing blow from the first wolf. Dakao hurled himself into the fray and killed both wolves with his spear, spinning like a weathervane in a storm.

The alpha flashed into the clearing, heading directly for me. I pointed the levitator at him and cranked the dial. Which would have been a great plan, but the beam missed, struck the ground, and it threw me backward through the air across the clearing. The wolf jumped to land on me. I engaged my left gauntlet's shield just in time, and he bounced off the glowing blue barrier.

The blow dazed the wolf, and he landed on his side with a whimper. I dove forward and wrenched the control box from his back. The wolf howled as the box came free, dragging blood and wires with it. He righted himself, shook his massive head, and ran toward the forest. He collapsed dead after only a few steps.

I limped back to the fight to find Dakao fending off the last of the wolves. I pointed to the levitator and carefully turned the dial. The wolf rose off the ground slowly, feet scrambling in mid-air. I pulled my belt knife and cut the control box from his back. Once it returned to its senses, I set the wolf back down and it ran off.

The bodies around the clearing told the story. Three dead Candalarians and eight dead wolves. Dakao knelt next to his fallen warriors.

"My fault. I broke the circle," he said as I stood next to

Gemaki's lifeless body. He picked up the nathal and threw it into the dark woods. "Evil has found us. You must stop this."

"What will you do?" I asked, hoping the big warrior would help me track down the Soul Stealer. It was obvious after this attack that it was not a one-man job. But from the look on his face, I knew he was returning home.

"I will take warriors back to families. It is duty."

I stood and left the grieving warrior to deal with his people.

Concern welled up inside me. Would Cian come back with reinforcements before I was attacked again? How could I hope to stop the people responsible for this by myself? I resolved to push forward and do the best I could do. It was what Roland would have done.

The only way forward was through.

The Candalarian warrior had the bodies of his deceased companions tied over the backs of their horses. I approached him to offer my help and express my gratitude and sorrow at the loss of his people. They'd refused to allow me to touch their fallen. Dakao helped me load the guard's corpses into the abandoned carriage so I could bring them back to civilization. He harnessed one of his pack horses to pull the rolling morgue.

"May your travels bring you to new places," Dakao said as he took my arm. "When next meet, may us not be enemies."

"Thank you," I said, not knowing how to respond to him. He pulled himself into his saddle and led the horses off to the south. I loaded the dead body of one of the wolves into the carriage with the men. I needed to be able to examine the attached control box.

The magus of Oriatia rode in comfort. Heavy steel springs supported the white and gold carriage. I thought about all the needless loss. All I could do now was make sure the guard's families could say goodbye, and I'd have intact devices to study. I searched every inch of the clearing for anything I'd missed but came up empty.

After the search, I put on my Watcher's robe and mask, since I needed to deposit the carriage and corpses with the authorities. Once I'd tied my horse and the pack animal to the carriage and checked the tethered team I was ready. I climbed into the driver's seat and set off toward Bexley's Crossing.

The trip took no time at all, including a stop to hide the wolf carcass outside town. Much sooner than I was ready for, I encountered the appointed Sheriff of Bexley's Crossing, Aaron Inchcombe. His thin, grey hair draped over his bald head, though it did little to hide his scalp. His long handlebar mustache had gone completely white, and his circular glasses were chipped in a couple of places. He eyed me up and down as I stood in the center of his office.

"So, you be a Watcher?" he asked, scorn coating every word like grease on a ball bearing. "Why not take the bodies and the coach back to her Eminence the Lady Pelham in Datchery?"

"Sheriff Inchcombe, I am a member of Arch Magus Everard's Watchers, not an errand boy. It is my responsibility to return these men to the local authorities, which is you." My voice sounded very different coming through my mask, lending it a properly menacing tone. "You will assign one of your people to return the carriage to Lady Pelham and deliver a note from me explaining what I found."

The sheriff pulled his pants up, but the girth of his belly made them retreat south as soon as he let go of them. "Well, Watcher…" When I didn't supply a name, he continued. "I'm not in the position—"

I'd had enough. I raised my left arm and turned the dial on the levitator. A trickle of icy energy raced down my arm. This close there was no missing, and the sheriff squawked like a startled goose as he rose into the air. Behind my mask, I grinned like a schoolboy who'd filched a pie. "You will do as I ask or I will replace you, understood?"

Inchcombe's arms and legs flailed as he tried to free himself from the levitator to no avail. He stammered out, "I agree, now put me down."

I turned off the levitator and let him land. Hard. Patience wasn't in my toolkit today.

The sheriff stumbled as he hit the wooden floor, grabbing his desk to steady himself. "Ya didn't need to do that. I'll get a couple of the boys to return the carriage." He glared at me as he said it.

I produced the note I'd written and handed it to him. The Watcher seal was evident, but I didn't trust the sheriff. "If the seal is broken by anyone other than Pelham, they'll die."

He dropped the paper onto the desk as if it was a snake. "I'll take care of it, sir."

I pivoted on my heel and ignored the itching between my shoulder blades. I was sure he'd love to shove a knife there, but I'd scared him enough to keep him in line. At least the levitator had worked correctly and I had better aim. I strode out of the sheriff's office, mounted my horse, hooked the lead rope of the packhorse to the pommel, and rode back to where the wolf carcass was stashed.

An hour later, I reached the hiding spot and cooked a quick lunch of bacon and beans. The flame attachment on my arm made starting a fire much easier than flint and steel. While I ate, I considered my plan to craft a device to track the nathal.

In Bexley's Crossing, I could probably find a blacksmith that would allow me to rent space from him. If I could craft the device I needed here, it would save a lot of time. After cleaning up and dousing the fire, I concealed all my Watcher-specific gear and entered the town from the far side.

I smelled the forge smoke before I saw the smithy. The complex sat on the edge of town, which suited my purposes. Everything looked to be well maintained and orderly, just the way I'd been taught. I tied the horses to an iron ring embedded in the wall over a watering trough and walked into the forge.

"Silas, work the bellows, boy," I heard as the blacksmith shoved some dully glowing metal back into the fire. "Silas, boy, get over here."

I went to the unmanned bellows and pushed them together slowly so as not to throw sparks or impede the fire. The rhythm of the work came naturally to me after so many years of being an apprentice. It felt like I'd returned home and I felt my mind clear and focused on the task at hand.

"When did you learn to control the fire like that? Yesterday, you just about set the place ablaze." The blacksmith clearly hadn't spotted me yet. I smiled as I continued. The blacksmith was a smaller man than I was but built like a bear. Thick arms, covered in tattoos, turned the metal in the forge as he waited for it to reach temperature. He pulled the billet from the fire and took the three-pound hammer to it, bending it around the horn of the anvil into a rough horseshoe shape. He kept at it until the metal cooled and then he replaced it in the fire.

"Da, there be a dead wolf out here!" A boy of about twelve ran into the forge, yelling at the blacksmith. Unless my guess was wrong, that would be Silas.

The blacksmith's head came up, and he noticed me working the bellows. "Silas, get over here. The fine gent shouldn't be doing yer job fer ya." The blacksmith walked over to where I stood as Silas took over the bellows. "Thank ye fer the help. I'm Matthew Redsmith. Can I assist ya with something?"

"Name's Zeke Smith," I said. "I'd like to rent some space to build a piece."

A frown crossed his bearded face. "I'm not much fer rentin' out my place. I've not got time fer teachin' you how to smith."

I pointed to the horseshoe in the fire. "May I?"

"Guessin' you mean to either way," he said, but the smile on his face told me he thought I'd make a fool of myself. Lots of people assume blacksmithing is just banging a hammer on metal. "Silas, can you work the pump?"

The boy clamped the bellows together, the flames leaping from the flood of air. No wonder his father had been so startled by Silas' 'improvement'. Master Redsmith demonstrated how to ease the air into the forge. The flare of sparks subsided and I set to work.

The metal had heated to glowing, so I pulled it out with the tongs and asked the smith, "Do you have a jig for this or are you hand bending it?" I already knew the answer, but I wanted to show my experience.

"Hand forging is the only way to get them right," he said with a smirk. We both understood it wasn't the case. If he'd been a farrier and shoed a lot of horses, he'd have a form to bend the metal around. I took the time to properly shape the shoe and drifted the nail holes. When it was perfect, I set the piece on the anvil to let it cool.

Master Redsmith examined the shoe, picking it up with the tongs. Rule number one in the forge —never pick up a piece of metal by hand. Hot metal looks the same as stone-cold, but the mistake has cost new smiths a lot of burnt fingers over the years. He set it back. "You know yer way around the forge. I could use some help instead of the rent."

Usually, I'd have jumped at the chance to work with a master smith, but time was of the essence. "I wish I could, but I need to forge my piece and be off." I pulled a gold coin from my pouch and tossed it to him. It would take him months to earn that much. He tossed it back.

"I don't take money from a fellow smith for usin' what's here. You wanna start now or in the morn?"

My brain said now, my body tomorrow. My body won the fight. "In the morning."

He smiled. "You look tuckered out. Head three doors down and tell Olivia I sent ya'. She'll put you up. She'll have supper on before long and you look like you could use a good meal."

I thanked him and followed his directions after laying the wolf out behind the forge where a casual passerby wouldn't see. An hour later, I sat at a table, enjoying a bowl of stew and a mug of ale. I'd examined the pistol I'd built to disrupt the communication device. The magic still flowed through it, but when the trigger broke it didn't discharge. Apparently, the function of the piece was as important as the magic tied to it. I pondered on if I reinforced the —

Without warning the door to the common room opened and Victoria Wyndham strolled through.

Of all the run-down inns in the world, why was she here?

"Phineas Overclock, I don't believe my eyes. You've returned from the Southern Tier and quite unexpectedly as well," Victoria said for all to hear as she crossed the dimly lit room.

I ducked my head and sank deeper into my seat. She practically danced toward my table. Luckily, I was in the back of the room, so everyone got a good look at her. She wore a purple paisley coat over a teal green blouse and dark pants with knee-high boots. Her dark hair was pulled up in an elaborate set of combs, and her goggles hung from around her neck like a statement piece. The clack of her boot heels echoed through the stunned silence of the small inn. Everard himself couldn't have made a grander entrance.

"Will you sit down?" I hissed through clenched teeth. "I'm going by Zeke Smith."

Her smile was that of pure sugar. "So I've heard. Stashing an armored wolf behind the smithy has gained more attention than you would guess. Phineas is a renowned explorer of the occult and famous for going undercover on his adventures. Would you rather be known as the eccentric adventurer or some sort of lunatic toting around dead animals?"

I rubbed my face as the day caught up with me. She wasn't done by a country mile.

"On top of that, Sheriff Inchcomb is telling everyone about the Watcher that appeared and cursed him for not assisting him fast enough." She tsked. "You have the manners of a sow, my young friend. Everard must see something in you to keep you around, but we definitely need to polish you up a bit."

"Is it really that bad?" I took a large swallow of ale, hoping it would wash away the stinging rebuke Victoria had just delivered.

She flipped her hand at me. "No, but it could have been. I decided to mention to the sheriff the newcomer to town was none other than the world-renowned adventurer Phineas Overclock. The incident with that nasty Watcher was gone in the blink of an eye. Our good sheriff is a huge fan."

"Is Phineas a real person?" I asked, taking another pull on my ale. The serving lass skipped over and set another mug on the table. "The gents at the bar sent this over." She glanced around conspiratorially. "Is it true you captured a giant crocodile and rode it to escape the Talu?"

Before I could answer, Victoria dove into the breach. "Actually, it was a sea serpent, but the editors didn't think people would believe the tale. The Talu still call him the Serpent God."

My jaw hung open at the audacity of the lie. "Well…"

She patted my hand like I was a slow child. "Phineas is shy about his adventures, which is why I follow him and chronicle his deeds. Otherwise, the world would never know of the exploits he gets himself into."

The maid's eyes grew wide as barrel rings. "Humble and

cute. If I do say so." She leaned in and kissed my cheek before scampering off behind the bar to a chorus of cheers and catcalls.

"See? No one will remember the strange man and ask questions. You've hidden in plain sight. There is a time and place for subterfuge and times for boldness."

I couldn't think of anything to say so I shoveled another bite of the spiced stew into my mouth and followed it with a swig of ale. Victoria's grin widened as the silence stretched on.

"You are so much fun to play with." She stole my fresh mug and sipped. "Not bad for the backwoods of Oriatia. Now, fill me in on what you've been doing, since I have some very interesting things to share with you."

The next half an hour I went over what had happened with Cian, the Candalarians, and the wolves. I ran down my plan to craft a device to track the nathal once I'd examined the wolf. She prodded my story, eliciting more information or shaking a detail loose I'd overlooked in the chaos of the fight.

"Interesting. I need to see the levitator work," she said as she tapped her finger on her chin, looking more like the Victoria I'd met in Stillhold than the peacock I sat across from now. "You don't strike me as the type to make mistakes in design. Before we're in a fight, you need to know why it malfunctioned."

"We?"

She reached over the table and patted my cheek. "Dear boy, you will definitely need help with this, and if you think I'm missing such a grand adventure, you've sorely underestimated me."

"No, ma'am," I replied out of habit.

She laughed. "Lady Eloise York appreciates your understanding, Phineas."

I laughed as well. Victoria's wild sense of humor was infectious and much needed after everything that had happened.

"After you left, I returned to my lab and ran more extensive tests on the drug and broke it down into how I believe it was synthesized. I attempted to trace the components back to the source. Two elements of the drug aren't available in Astaria. One I found with a Candalarian merchant who smuggles the substance into Iron Harbor, but the other comes from the jungles of Uwhela."

"Uwhela? I've never heard of such a place."

"I'd be surprised if you had. Uwhela is south of Candalar. It's mostly jungle and the home of the Talu. They're cannibals and use human sacrifices to power their magic. Nasty place, but if we are to stop this drug from coming into Astaria, we need to find where it is coming from."

"You mean we need to travel through Candalar, find a cannibal mage, and stop them from creating the hypnotic drug?" I shook my head in disbelief. "Not much to it, huh?"

"Not we, me," she said with a grin. "I fabricated the drug without the unknown element. While it is an excellent sedative, it does not lead to the overwhelming hypnotic effect of the substance used on the animals. Now you probably need both the drug and the nathal to control an animal, but it's a start."

"How do you know that?"

"A bird flew into the lab and told me, of course," she said with a smirk. "Why, I took the drug and had my apprentice Letitia command me to do things. My version had no effect, though I did want to fall asleep."

"You tested the drug on yourself?" I asked a bit more sharply than I'd meant to.

Victoria rolled her eyes. "Science demands risk. I was

fairly sure there was no danger, and I needed to know if it worked like the original."

"You didn't take the original, did you?"

"Of course. Letitia had a fine laugh as she made me cluck like a chicken and do some silly folk dance. Afterward, I had her clean every bit of our lab equipment, but she was still laughing."

"Are you crazy?" I asked, appalled that she would risk her life, sanity, and health on a drug being used to turn animals into killing machines. "What if you had turned violent and harmed your apprentice?"

"She had a syringe of sedative and a loaded pistol if it came to that. As I hypothesized, the animals only turn violent when instructed to, and Letitia was to not give any command that could be construed that way."

"The more you try, the more you do," I said, reciting a favorite quote of my mentor Roland. When I made mistakes, which was often, he would tell me that.

Victoria cocked her head. "Where did you hear that?"

"Roland. He said it a lot during my training."

"I haven't heard that since his previous apprentice died years ago."

I frowned. "I didn't know Roland had another apprentice."

"Mortimer was his apprentice before you. He died in a fire trying to rescue a family. It took Roland a long time to quit blaming himself."

Knowing Roland, he'd never gotten over it, just hidden it better. I'd have to ask Jabber about Mortimer when I got back to Treetop. For now, I needed to forge a locater to find the person behind these attacks. I fought down a yawn.

"It's late and we need to start early," I said as I pushed away from the table.

"What did the mother cow say to her baby cow?"
I rubbed my forehead, waiting for the answer.
"It's pasture bedtime."
I groaned and left the common room to find my bed.

In the morning, I descended the stairs and found Victoria seated near the door, book in hand, waiting on me. The sun had only been up for a few minutes. Did she ever sleep?

"Morning," I said as I crossed the room. The place smelled of sweat, stale beer, and burnt stew. She stood to greet me. Today, she wore a leather vest over a grey shirt and pants, the tops of which were stuffed into her boots. Her hair was pulled back into a ponytail.

"Let's go." She turned on her heel on headed out the front door. I followed along, too tired comment on her appropriating my mission to stop the attacks. She'd proven to be smart and flexible. I could do far worse in a partner.

We walked in silence, rounding the smithy to retrieve the wolf. I pulled the corpse away from the building and pried the top of the control box off so we could see the inside of the device. The same syringe of the blue drug rode next to a larger device similar to the first, but I could feel the magic rolling off this one like clouds churning over a lake. I'd missed the magic signature on the original. My skills must be making me more sensitive to magic in general.

"So that is a nathal?" Victoria asked as she probed the inner workings of the metal container. The copper tubes ran forward toward the brain, as did the wires. I followed the visible scar until it reached the ears. When I turned the wolf's head, it revealed a device embedded in the ear canal. After a bit of fishing, I retrieved a small piece of metal, inscribed like the piece in the control box.

Victoria picked it up. "This must be how they told it what to do."

The idea of an animal being able to understand so many human commands struck me as unlikely, but two attacks later what else could it be? "At least we know how they are coordinating the attacks."

"This is barbaric. To what possible end could they be using these poor animals to harm people?

"Every ambush has been in a place where a magus should have been. The bear attacked the towns where it killed the Watcher and one where Magus Hoadley of Aldon had been the day before. Magus Pelham had been scheduled to be in the carriage the wolves ambushed. Either someone knows about the devices the magi use or they are trying to eliminate the magus of the southern regions." I still couldn't produce an argument for either hypothesis. Neither made a lot of sense since the control boxes on these animals far surpassed anything the magus carried. How could magus be a threat to people who knew how to create this sophisticated magic?

"I feel we are missing something." She traced the scars along the back of the wolf's neck with her finger. "This is a merging of flesh, magic, and technology. Whoever is behind this has an advanced understanding of things you and I are just touching on. Given enough time they could control Astaria itself."

Which made my mission to find this person or people and put an end to it even more urgent. After that, we could establish if they were after the magic artifacts or another reason.

Victoria stood and I did the same. "Can you really create a device to locate these people?"

"I think I can," I said, wishing I was more confident in my abilities. My failure of using the levitator during the fight had rattled me. "I still haven't figured how I missed with the levitator."

She stepped back from me and spread her arms wide. "Lift me."

Of course, Victoria would volunteer instead of pointing out an object that couldn't feel pain. Of course, I hadn't asked the Sherrif and he'd been fine after. I did as she requested, though. I raised my left arm, aimed, and slowly turned the dial. She rose smoothly into the air. For the next few minutes, Victoria put me through my paces. Left, right, up, down, push, and pull. The whole time she clapped and laughed at the experience.

"Set me down gently, please."

She bumped on the ground and joined me. "Lift the wolf."

I did and it floated into the air before returning just as gently.

Victoria clapped me on the shoulder. "It seems to work. Try lifting the wagon."

I pointed and turned the dial. I felt an immense pressure pushing down on me. After a few seconds of the wagon not budging the pressure turned to pain as I sunk into the ground. I twisted the dial to off and the pain subsided.

"You're a bit shorter than I remember," Victoria said with a wry tone in her voice.

My knees were even with the dirt now. "It looks like I can't lift anything heavier than I am."

Victoria helped me out of the hole I'd created. "Well, that illuminates a few things. During the fight, you said you missed the target?"

"I assume so," I said hesitantly. In the chaos of the fight, I wasn't sure what had happened. "The force threw me across the clearing."

She tapped her chin as she thought. "Try pointing at the ground and see what happens."

I did, turning the dial carefully controlling the lift. This time, I was the one who rose in the air as the force of the magic pushed against me. My spirits rose along with my body. I had created magic and it worked. All those months I thought I was a failure. and now I was levitating both other things and myself with my own power.

The things I would be able to do with this—like fly! If I added a attachment it would let me—

"Quinn, play time is over. Now be a good sport and come down from there."

Reluctantly, I turned the dial to off and landed on the ground.

She shrugged. "It makes sense. You don't have the leverage to move the earth, so the force rebounds against you.With the wagon you were exerting an upward force, thus you sank. Luckily, you weren't standing on stone or you'd have broken your legs. The faster you turn the dial, the more violent the repulsion."

"This will come in handy when we find who is behind all this," I said trying to not sound over proud of myself.

"You've definitely piqued my curiosity." She cleared her throat. "But none of this gets us closer to stopping these attacks."

"Right." I headed for the smithy. The master blacksmith was already hammering away at a shovel head. Up with the light was how smiths worked. I greeted him as did Victoria.

I waited for him to place the shovel into the fire before I interrupted further. "I need to build a piece and will require the forge. It is truly life or death, but I don't want to cost you trade by delaying your work."

"I appreciate the thought, but I'll be fine. I've heard rumors and wild stories about you. The whole town is abuzz. Don't matter though. You're a fellow blacksmith and I'd be honored for you to use my forge."

"We would be happy to pay you for your time," Victoria added, but I shot her a look as the smith's face darkened. He had already refused payment and she was insulting him, albeit unknowingly.

"I appreciate your generosity," I said over her before she made things worse. She might be an expert on the outside world, but I knew the smithy. "What can I do in return?"

"I've been thinking since our talk last night. If you'd come back and help me catch up, I'd be in your debt," Master Redsmith said.

"Consider it done. Once I finish the next portion of my journey, I'd be proud to work by your side," I said, all the while wondering if I'd live to fulfill this promise.

"I'll be your assistant for as long as you need me, master smith." He pulled the piece he'd been heating and set it aside, freeing the forge for me.

Without more words, I started to work. I took the nathal out and placed it on the anvil, feeling the magic flowing from it. The magic drifted off to the east, the path almost visible when I concentrated on it. I picked a piece of metal stock and trickled magic into it. Once it was charged I set it in the coal forge. I didn't want any awkward questions about forging "cold" metal. Master Redsmith worked the bellows, fetched tools, and assisted with the finer details as I bent my will to find where the magic came from. Victoria sat on a bench, out of the way, watching like a hawk.

While the metal heated in the forge, I found a slender piece of iron and crafted three pins to repair the pistol. I'd need it for this adventure, I was sure. Once that was done, I returned to the tracking device.

The sun had just started to set over the mountains as I put the pieces together. The pointer on the crude compass never wavered from what I believed was the source of the magic controlling the animals. If it worked, we could put an end to these senseless killings, but that was a giant if.

I thanked Master Redsmith for his assistance and we returned to the inn. I barely made it to my room before I collapsed into an exhausted sleep. Working with magic was far more draining than just using the fire and hammer. Tomorrow we'd track the person responsible for these attacks.

I only hoped we were up to the task of defeating them.

22

An hour before sunrise when I silently entered the common room, Victoria already lounged by the common room's door, bright as the morning sun. She cast me a cheeky smile as if she knew I'd been trying to arrive before her this time.

"Good morning," I said.

"The horses are saddled out front and I've seen to the provisions for the mission. I refuse to eat the jerky you live on."

I ignored the comment and thanked her before we mounted up. Victoria sat astride her horse with the pack-horse tethered to her pommel. She'd packed enough for three missions from the looks of it. I checked the compass and it still pointed east.

I tapped my horse's flank and we headed out as the sun crept up from the horizon. We crossed the bridge over the Itugar River, guided by the compass. Victoria rode by my side as we left the road and entered the forest.

After a couple of hours, we came across a game trail. I wished Cian were here to identify the tracks, but to me, they looked like a mixture of horse hooves and paw prints. It was as good of a sign as any. The compass pointed in the general direction of the trail so we stayed on course.

"Do you have a plan for when we find the people responsible? If you don't I have a few ideas." Victoria asked. The birds sang as we rode, which was a good sign since during the attacks the forest had gone silent.

"I won't until we see what we're up against. Who knows what other animals they've perverted? And they may have magic we haven't seen yet. What are you carrying for weapons?"

She slid matching pistols from under her coat. I'd seen similar ones back at the workshop, but they weren't the new models Cian wielded. "I always come prepared for trouble."

I checked the compass again and it wobbled back and forth, reorienting. We must be close. After an hour, we spotted a small compound of buildings set in a valley below the ridge we had just crested.

Victoria produced a pair of binoculars and studied the scene before handing them over. Men armed with swords and clubs walked between the buildings. There was a large whitewashed house in the foreground. The shutters were missing, or hanging loose, giving the impression it had been abandoned long ago. A massive barn, its once red paint faded to grey, stood behind the house. One of the doors lay off to the side near a dilapidated shed. Two wagons sat outside the barn doors, loaded with cages containing wolves and a small bear, probably a cub from the size.

"This looks to be the place," I said as I handed back the binoculars. "Do we ride down and take them out?"

She shook her head. "We are outnumbered, and if they release the animals, even more so. There must be at least ten armed guards and who knows how many others? We need to attack at night so we have the element of surprise."

I hated to delay, but she was right. After I tethered my horse and removed the saddlebags. Behind the deadfall tree was a good place to watch while we waited for the sun to go down. Victoria rifled through her pack pulling out bottles filled with a variety of colored powders.

"What are you doing?"

She didn't look up as she continued her search. "I thought it might be a good idea to have a couple of tricks on hand."

"Surprises are good," I said as I pulled out my toolkit to adjust my gear. "As long as they are surprises for them, not us."

I put a new piece of alarium in my arm. If my arm went dead in the middle of a fight, it wouldn't be so great for me. I checked the shield, fire, and lightning weapons to make sure they were operational. The levitator and the broken disrupter pistol wouldn't need alarium—only my magic, as miraculous as that seemed.

"Rest assured, I am well versed in fighting," Victoria said with a wicked grin.

After seeing her drop the three toughs at the inn, I had no doubt, though she looked more like a librarian than a fighter. I retrieved the pins I'd made at Master Redsmith's forge and repaired the disruptor pistol. Then I set to carving a couple of wooden stakes. You could never be too prepared.

Victoria continued mixing potions, sitting across from me, behind a fallen log. "You know how good things come to those who wait?"

"They do?"

"Yep, unless you're waiting on death."

When would I learn not to ask?

23

The hours crept by as we watched the people of the compound go about their business. We ate from the provisions Victoria had purchased and I hated to admit they were much better than what I'd brought. The farmhouse bell rang announcing dinner. We needed the darkness to help us fight so many men.

As darkness fell, Victoria took her pistols and checked the sights for the fourth time. We both wore our Watchers masks, so we were able to see in the darkness of the new moon. When the lamps were extinguished in the main house, we put our plan in motion.

"I'll take care of the house, you lock down the barn so we don't have to fight any more animals," I told her as we descended the slope toward the compound.

"Affirmative," she replied as we separated to handle our tasks.

We hadn't seen any additional people join the ranks of the camp below. Security was definitely lax given how long we'd been here and not one person patrolled the treeline. Given the distance to any roads, I doubted anyone was worried about intruders. At least I hoped so. Between my armaments and Victoria's pistols, we should be able to handle anyone who tried to stop us, but my confidence fled when it came to the animals hopped up on the control drugs.

I reached the farmhouse as Victoria slid through the night toward the barn. Up close, it was plain the whitewash had flaked off long ago. Two windows flanked the front door. I stalked around the house to the back where I found another exit. As quietly as possible, I wedged the spikes I'd cut between the door and the jam to stop anyone from leaving this way. Once I was satisfied, I set fire to the rear of the house and ran to the front. The ancient structure went up like a soot-filled chimney from the ball of fire I threw at it. I stood off to the side of the front door and waited.

Screams of panic erupted inside as the fire spread through the derelict house. The front door slammed open. A worker ran out into the night and I shocked him with a lightning blast from my gauntlet, knocking him out cold. I repeated the process on the second and third men who fled, but my luck ran out as I shocked the fourth man. The man behind him leapt over the prone form and landed beyond my reach. While I tried to fire on him, three more emerged, pulling knives and swords when they saw me.

The first swung his short sword at me, but I blocked it with my metal arm. He dropped the sword from the impact, cursing loudly as his compatriot charged in with a knife. I hit him with a blast of flame followed by a swift kick to his crotch. He screamed as he fell off the porch, landing hard on the ground, clutching himself.

Another man darted in, a sword the ready when pain jabbed through my side just above the hip. A knife. The first man had awakened and charged in to join the melee. While it wasn't a deep cut, the wound burned along my side. I lost focus for a second, and the running man slammed into me, knocking me off the porch and onto the ground. The breath fled at the forces of the impact.

I had just caught my breath when a foot slammed into my injured side. I rolled away only to have another man dive on me. I wrestled with my attacker with a combination of metal arm and curses. I fired lightning at my opponent's head. He screamed as he reared back, grasping his ruined face. I rolled to the side, avoiding another kick as more people emerged from the burning building. I swept flames at them to keep them at a distance.

The sound of breaking glass and coughing came from behind me. I glanced back to see a cloud surrounding two of the men who were in the process of vomiting on the ground. A third man screamed as a slug from Victoria's pistol took him in the shoulder. The other two rushed me.

I activated my shield, stopping the bigger man's sword strike. I lashed out, catching my other opponent under the chin with a metal fist. A loud crack accompanied the blow. He fell backward and lay still. I fired a bolt of lightning into the sword-wielding man, knocking him out.

Victoria ran over. "We've got a big problem."

I looked over her shoulder and saw what she meant. Cian turned the corner, two wolves flanking him as he stalked toward us.

"Quinn, come with me, and I'll let her go," he said. He stood holding the struggling alchemist about ten feet from where I was.

"You've got to fight the hypnosis," Victoria said. "We'll find whoever did this to you."

Cian threw back his head and laughed. His mask hung around his neck, swaying as he mocked Victoria. "You think I'm being controlled? Don't be stupid."

"You're a Watcher," I said, "How could you betray your duty? We protect the people of Astaria."

"The Watchers are Everard's toys and he doesn't care if we are broken, he just gets new ones. All we do is keep the false magus in power. Once Everard is gone, we'll take over and use the alarium to destroy Candalar once and for all. Then the people of Astaria will be safe."

It suddenly made sense why they were doing this. "The attack on Lapis was to steal the alarium from the magus' arm piece?"

Cian laughed again. "You think you're so smart, but you need the truth spelled out for you. You will build us the weapons to eliminate the Candalarians and the Norns. Astaria will take its rightful place in the world."

"You're a traitor." Victoria spat at his feet. "We don't negotiate with your ilk."

Cian grinned. "You always thought too much of yourself, Victoria." He pointed at us and commanded the wolves: "Attack."

I recognized the alpha from our earlier fight, an ambush I now knew Cian had orchestrated. Lady Pelham's guards had been slaughtered so I would investigate with only Cian by my side, but the arrival of the Candalarians had messed up his plans.

I was a fool.

Victoria and I pivoted so our backs were protected by the other. The wolves ran at us. The alpha leapt at me, but I knocked it away with my fist. Victoria fell beneath the other wolf. The animal pressed down, teeth snapping as it sought to rip out her throat. I kicked it in the side, driving it off her. The alpha darted in from behind and cut my legs out from under me. I went down hard as it landed on my back.

"Just say the word and I'll call them off." Cian's voice was harsh. "Why die to protect Everard?"

"I honor my word," Victoria said as she kicked the attacking wolf in the jaw.

I struggled to my knees but the alpha pounced, knocking me to the ground again. He pulled at the leather hood of my cloak which, thankfully, blocked my neck for the time being. I pushed my arm into the ground, readying to levitate myself. The wolf's paw knocked the dial out of my hand before I could turn the dial.

I swore as the wolf tore at the material blocking him from my neck. My hand found the dial and I twisted it. Magic surged into me, taking my breath away. With a blast of blue energy, the magic shot me and the wolf straight up into the air at an accelerated rate.

After a few seconds, I turned off the dial which did two things. First, the wolf kept rising, as its momentum wasn't tied to the device but to my body. Second, I fell.

From my new vantage point, I spotted Cian racing toward Victoria who still fought with the other wolf. I engaged the levitator to slow my descent. I threw a fireball at Cian to prevent him from reaching Victoria. He danced away from the flame as I landed feet first with a thump.

Cian threw a knife at Victoria, clipping her shoulder as she dodged, but it was enough of a distraction. The wolf pounced, driving her to the ground. She shoved her arms against its neck, but she didn't have the strength to hold it off. Cian sauntered up, pulling his swords from their sheathes. I was too far away to reach her, and she'd be hurt by anything from my arm. I grabbed the disruptor pistol from my belt and fired it at the wolf.

Nothing happened. Again.

Frustration crashed on me and I threw the useless pistol at the wolf. It struck it in the side and exploded with light.

The effects were immediate. The wolf stopped snapping at its prone victim. After a great shake of its head, it fled into the night, leaving a scratched and bloodied Victoria behind.

I dropped to my knees as the same overwhelming cold as

before enveloped me. My teeth chattered as my body shook uncontrollably. I forced myself to my feet. My mechanical arm spasmed as the connection failed.

Cian sprinted across the space between us. His long sword arced in, overhand, and I jerked to the side. It clanged against the metal of my arm. Cian kicked me, throwing my balance off. My arm detached, crashing to the dirt. The lack of weight caused me to overbalance and land on my side avoiding the short sword thrust.

I heard another bottle break near my feet, releasing billowing smoke. With the Watcher's mask, I was safe, but Cian hadn't been wearing his. He retreated, coughing as the vapor found his lungs. The thick smog obscured my vision but gave me time to shake off the freezing effects of the magic. I tugged on the straps and restored my arm to full use.

A form appeared in front of me and I barely had time to block Cian's sword as it arced overhead. He'd gotten his mask on before the fumes had overcome him. We now fought in a swirling mass of smoke. Pain flared in my good arm as the short sword bit into my gauntlet. Something broke and blood flowed down my arm, but I couldn't pay it any attention.

I jumped back to avoid a strike that would have gutted me but snagged on the leather strap of my pouch. It gave me the opening I needed. I grabbed the sword with my metal hand and snapped it off the hilt. Cian released the sword, jumped up, and drove both feet into my chest, sending me backward out of the smoke. I hit with a jarring thud and felt my arm loosen. The sensation flickered as the connections yet again lost contact with my skin. I needed to use my magic to attach my arm so it would stop falling off.

Cian stalked out of the fog, short sword in his hand and blood lust in his eyes. When he noticed my hand spasming, he smiled. "I'll be taking the alarium now, Quinn."

I tried to push myself up with the semi-attached arm but collapsed. I was a fish out of water with the hawk bearing down on me.

Thud.

Cian crumpled, revealing Victoria right behind him, pistol gripped like a club.

"Well, he's certainly a knockout," Victoria said.

I groaned, but somehow we'd won.

It didn't feel like a victory.

24

Victoria helped me reattach my arm and bandaged my elbow where Cian had cut through my gauntlet. That treacherous bastard, now trussed up like a pig ready for the spit, was still unconscious from the knock on the head. The freed animals had already fled. We tied the arms and legs of the men who'd been helping Cian. After we removed Cian's weapons, Victoria confiscated his mask, checking his eyes.

He moaned as she prodded his skull harder than necessary. "Don't seem to be any fractures, so he'll recover. I have just the thing to encourage his cooperation." She rummaged through her bag, examining each until she found what she wanted. After all the fighting, I was amazed they weren't broken.

Cian stirred and I pointed his own pistol at him. "You've got a lot to answer for."

He looked up at me with bleary eyes. "You stopped me, but there are more to finish the job."

"Yes," Victoria said brightly. "And this will make you feel really friendly and want to help us."

He shook his head. "I know all about your tricks, Victoria." He opened his hand to show a syringe of the blue drug. He shoved the needle into his leg and depressed the plunger before I could stop him. His head sagged back as he passed out.

"Is he dead?" I asked as Victoria tried to rouse him.

"He's still breathing. Too much of the drug can kill you. I don't know if there was enough there to overdose on."

"Dead men tell no tales."

Victoria nodded. Cian was alive but non-responsive. she tried again to awaken him, but he stayed absent. "I'll have to make an antidote first. For that I have to find the compound in its pure form," she said once she'd finished with Cian.

"He wasn't doing this alone. We need to find the other people behind this and stop them," I argued. "Cian may recover and tell us. I'll take him back to Treetop and Jabber can nurse him back to health or maybe Everard could use magic to "persuade" him to help us find the people behind this."

She snorted. "Everard can stop an invading army, but delicate work to remove the effects of this drug are beyond him. I'll travel to Uwhela, find who created the compound, and destroy their ability to do so. If Cian stays alive long enough after the overdose, the antidote may bring him back to answer for what he's done."

"Aren't you being hasty?" I asked, not wanting her to go, at least without me. Just as my task had, in the end, required her help, perhaps hers would require help as well. "He could recover in a few days."

"You can handle him if he does. Regardless, I have to destroy the manufacturer of the compound or we'll never be free of this drug. You think there won't be more people willing to create mindless slaves to do their bidding?"

She was right and we both knew it. She packed away her

things. "I'll be in touch when I return. You'll have to stop the upcoming attacks, but at least you can warn the magus about the dangers."

I nodded. "Be careful and good luck."

"I'm always careful." She turned to leave but then faced me. "You know the problem with a two-headed horse?"

"No."

"You can never tell if it's coming or going." She laughed.With a smirk and a wave, she left to start her mission. I'd miss her jokes. Well, maybe not a lot. And off Victoria went. I wondered if the people she hunted were ready for her.

I seriously doubted it. She angled for the tree line where we'd secured our horses. I'd use Cian's horse to tote him back to Treetop. As I sat on the ground next to Cian, I realized he'd broken my levitator when he struck my gauntlet. I'd have to remake it since there were a lot of other uses for it, like putting an unconscious man on the back of his horse.

The groans of the other men roused me from my thoughts. I loaded Cian and the men into one of the wagons and set off for Bexley's Crossing. As the sun rose, I rode toward the town so I could turn them over to the authorities.

The longer journey would be in stopping whoever was behind this whole plan in order to protect the people of Astaria.

Because that was what Watchers did.

THE END

AFTERWORD

You are holding in your hands a book I seriously wondered if I'd ever publish. I finished the draft and sent it off to my editor, the incredible Jody Wallace. She sent the revisions back and the next week COVID struck. Writing went on the back burner as we all struggled with our new "reality." Frankly, it sucked for me, for you, and for everyone we all know. After losing friends who are truly missed, writing a steampunk book didn't seem so important.

After a year of isolation, and completing every jigsaw puzzle known to man, I realized, with my wife's encouragement, I had to reconnect with my creative process for my own sanity. It took a while. Jody had some amazing suggestions around strengthening the plot. We did a couple of passes and the book really came into shape. I am really proud of this book.

Meanwhile, life goes on. Both kids graduated (one from high school, one from college). I started a new job, as did my wife. Of course, Blaze, our super cute Cavalier, was thrilled that suddenly the entire family was home 24/7. He didn't even mind supervising everyone.

As with all good books, Of Cogs & Conjuring is the sum total of a lot of people's hard work in turning my storytelling into readable fiction. Jody Wallace is an amazing editor and a great sounding board for everything from cats to plot twists. Fortunately for all my readers, she'll be back to work on book 2 of the Watchers of Astaria. Natania Barron did the amazing cover art. I can't tell you the number of compliments I get about my covers. Betty Rose, my wonderful mom, did the proofread. They always tell you not to listen to your mom when she likes your writing, but mine was a profession proofreader so I lucked out having such a fantastic mom. Cheri and Chuck did the beta read on Cogs. They have been with me from the start and continue to point out stuff I've missed.

A special thank you to Laurel Anne Hill. She was the winner of the RavenCon Kickstarter to be red-shirted in Cogs. I hope I did her proud with her death scene.

Blaze wanted me to put him in this book because it wouldn't have been possible without his constant support and need for treats.

Our kids, Emily & Nicholas, are inspirations every day. They are both smart and kind people and I'm really proud of them. My wife, Hope, is the rock my life is built on. She is my best friend, an amazing wife, and my biggest cheerleader. Publishing books comes with a lot of rejection and frustration. She's always there to steady the ship and keep me looking at the good parts. I doubt I'd still be writing without her.

And lastly, thank you to all of you, my readers. Knowing that you enjoy and appreciate the work that goes into these books makes it all worthwhile. If you enjoy my books, the best thing you can do it tell a friend and post a review on Amazon.

Until next time,
Patrick
June 2021

ABOUT THE AUTHOR

Patrick Dugan is the author of the Darkest Storm Series. *Storm Forged,* his debut novel, won the 2019 Imadjinn Award for Best Indie Science Fiction novel. *Storm Forged* is a super-hero coming of age story with an innovative structure for both powers and politics that continues with *Unbreakable Storm* and concludes with *Storm Shattered. Of Cogs & Conjuring* Watchers of Astaria Book 1 and *Fate & Flux: A Steampunk Adventure,* feature Quinn, a one-armed blacksmith who goes on to become a Watcher to protect Astaria from numerous foes.

Patrick's love of all thing tech continues to drive him to write books that intertwine technology and magic to produce unique worlds and intriguing stories.

When there isn't a global pandemic, you can find Patrick at conventions around the Southeast, discussing writing, geek culture, and teaching writing tools as part of his role as Director of Technology Services with Author's Essentials.

Patrick lives with his wife, two children, and a spunky Cavalier King Charles Spaniel, named Blaze. When not writing, he loves to homebrew beer, 3D print all sorts of fun stuff, collect Funko Pops, and play video games, especially anything by Blizzard. You can find his Blood Elf Warlock roaming Azeroth most evenings.

You can find out more at www.patrickdugan.net, https://www.facebook.com/patrick.dugan.3781, https://www.instagram.com/patrickduganauthor/, https://twitter.com/P_Dugan

The Darkest Storm Series

Storm Forged

Unbreakable Storm

Storm Shattered

The Watchers of Astaria

Fate & Flux